USA TODAY BESTSELLING AUTHOR

Dale Mayer

HEROES FOR HIRE

STONE'S SURRENDER: HEROES FOR HIRE, BOOK 2
Beverly Dale Mayer
Valley Publishing Ltd.

ISBN-13: 978-1-773360-23-2
Print Edition

Books in This Series:

Carson's Choice: Heroes for Hire, Book 28
Dante's Decision: Heroes for Hire, Book 29
Steven's Solace: Heroes for Hire, Book 30

Boxed Sets and Bundles
https://geni.us/Bundlepage

About This Book

Welcome to *Stone's Surrender*, book 2 in Heroes for Hire reconnecting readers with the unforgettable men from SEALs of Honor in a new series of action packed, page turning romantic suspense that fans have come to expect from USA TODAY Bestselling author Dale Mayer.

Life is on the move again...

After a long slow-ass recovery, Stone finds himself triumphantly back at work at Levi's new company. The action comes fast and furious on his first run out as they rescue a senator's daughter who's been kidnapped in the Middle East.

Lissa will do almost anything to thwart her father's plans for her. Getting kidnapped wasn't on her list. And once she meets Stone no other man matters. She falls, and she falls hard. But even on home soil, there's no respite as she finds the nightmare has followed her home...and she's caught in the middle of it.

It's a battle that requires both of them to not only clear her name but to keep her safe...especially when a twist is thrown at them that they didn't see coming...

Sign up to be notified of all Dale's releases here!
https://geni.us/DaleNews

Chapter 1

"TWO MORE DAMN-CLOSE shots."

Stone Tollard winced, sitting taller in the driver's seat, as Levi swore loud and long into Stone's headset.

The next distinctive *boom* shook their vehicle. Stone turned to look at Ice, riding shotgun beside him.

"Stone, what's your ETA?" Levi's hard voice snagged Stone's attention. Levi and the rest of the unit arrived earlier in another truck and were already situated in town, scoping things out.

At least until Stone swerved to avoid another depression in the road. Likely a land mine again. He checked the laptop monitor mounted before him. Ice's main duty was watching this screen, although she'd rather be flying a helicopter. She nodded for him to continue in the same direction.

Normally this would be a military operation. Yet no one was to know Levi and his unit were in Afghanistan to rescue a senator's daughter—kidnapped by rebels intent on funding their army for another couple years. Not that the senator didn't have the money to pay, because he did; but, as everyone knew, paying was no guarantee of getting the senator's daughter home safe and sound. In the senator's own words, Lissa was a mite too stubborn to listen to anyone—even kidnapping rebels.

The senator knew what Levi could do and also trusted

him to keep this as quiet as possible. On those terms Levi had agreed to take on the job.

Levi's team were all ex-soldiers of some kind and excelled in this stuff, although there was talk of a few other law enforcement types joining them. One of Levi's old friends, Mike, a Texas Ranger, was looking to join up. Stone had no trouble with that because Mike had helped them out before, having access to some information and skills that they wouldn't have otherwise. Stone was all for a global company.

Hell, although the formal name of Levi's company was Legendary Security, privately the team joked their name should be *Heroes for Hire*. Truly sappy. And something to make them all groan. But anything to put a grin on their faces and to turn tough situations into something easier was well worth it.

"Now." Ice's voice rose sharply at the end of the word as she pointed where she wanted Stone to go.

Stone tightened his grip on the wheel and made a sharp left turn and kept going until she told him otherwise. Stone and Levi had learned to listen to Ice a long time ago.

"Straighten up," she said in a calm voice. "You're clear for another hundred yards."

"Jesus, is that all?" he asked.

No way in hell they'd have made it this far if they didn't have that special software. Although military grade, it was an early adaptation of Mason's partner, Tesla's, program. So technically not an illegal copy. More of a prototype, and she'd made a few tweaks to improve its efficiency and accuracy. Stone was damn grateful.

He and Ice would've been blown to shit a long time ago if they didn't have this thing telling them where all the land mines were. They couldn't be positive every single mark on that screen was one, but they sure as hell weren't taking any chances. The program had been developed to forewarn them, and it worked like a charm.

"Stone?" Levi asked impatiently. "ETA? Answer me."

Stone looked at Ice.

She shrugged. "If we could go in a straight line, it would be eight minutes," she said to both men. "Since we're zigzagging across the damn countryside to avoid land mines, double that."

Stone kept his focus on the road, knowing they neared the one-hundred-yard mark, and Ice would fire off another set of instructions soon.

"Clear so far."

He nodded. That meant in ten seconds she would tell him to head in another direction she deemed safe. And he'd follow her order, as he had for years. And it was so much easier now that she and Levi had settled their differences. When they'd been on the outs, it had been tough on everybody. The team could all see what needed to happen, but nobody dared speak to Levi or Ice since both were hotheads.

Stone grinned. Of course he was just a pussycat himself. *Like hell.*

He and Ice drove in silence for another couple minutes, and he was surprised when she didn't tell him to change direction. It also made him extremely uneasy. This was the longest they'd actually driven in a straight line since they'd hit this section of the road. "Is the program still working?"

"It is. And there's one coming up ninety yards to the right. Take a left in four, three, two …"

The cab was silent except for his heavy breathing as he waited for that final order.

"Now," she snapped.

He jerked the wheel again, making a hard left, and waited for her to tell him to straighten up. That meant heading back to the road when it was clear. But she didn't say anything. He glanced at her quickly and then returned his gaze to the road. The double-cab truck bounced over the heavy countryside, hit a rock, then bounced again. Not a whole lot he could do. The terrain was very rough out here.

"Ice?"

"Get ready," she warned. "When I say so, take a hard right and go forward about ten yards."

"Jesus." He followed her instructions though. It took another five minutes before she had them on the road again. And so it went for the next fifteen miles. At one point it seemed like nothing but land mines were on the road. Finally the small village rose up ahead. Not their final destination but where they would stay for the night. Lissa was being held somewhere within a few miles of this place.

He entered the village very slowly, dust swarming up around them.

Levi's voice crackled in his ear. "Take the second left."

Stone shook his head. There was no left, nor right because there were no damn roads. Just a hodgepodge of makeshift buildings set in the middle of nowhere. How the hell did these people live like this?

Ice lifted her hand and pointed to the left. He followed her instructions and came to a sudden stop inside what appeared to be a shelter of some kind. Instantly the men on the ground covered up the truck with camouflage materials. Stone hopped out and walked over to Rhodes and Merk, standing in front of the truck. For every step Stone took, he heard a *clink, clink, clink.*

Rhodes shook his head and looked down at Stone's foot and leg hidden by his jeans. "That won't work. No way can you sneak up on anybody like that."

"Two screws are loose. I just need a minute to fix it," Stone said.

Merk cleared a spot on the table and said, "Take that thing off, and I'll get to it."

Only ... Stone did things his way. He stood at the table, reached down, pulled up his pant leg, and took off his prosthetic leg. Then he laid it on the clean spot on the table. Instantly a light turned on, giving him visibility as bright as he could get here. Tools were all over the place; few of them belonged to his team. But Stone would use what he could. Quickly checking out the offending joint, he realized one of the bearings was working less than perfectly.

He always carried a repair kit in his pocket, just in case. He pulled that out, quickly changed the seal and replaced the screws, taking great care to oil everything. Soon as he was done, he strapped it on again. This model had a butter-soft leather pad for his stump and was much easier on the scar tissue.

His buddy, Swede, had helped him design a different clip-on system. All in all each new design was getting better and better. None were as good as the flesh-and-blood leg he'd lost, but he was doing just fine.

At least until he was all alone in the dark. Sometimes the waves of depression just couldn't be held back. But those were few and far between, and he sure as hell would never admit those times to anybody else. That would be surrendering, admitting to the weakness within. He'd never done that. Not yet at least, and didn't have any plans to do so in the near future.

He swung around to the others and asked, "What's the plan?"

"You and Ice will take the road up to the rear of the rebel camp on the other side of those hills. We want you to park at the top and be the lookout. Harrison's going with you. Sniper rifles are right over there on the left wall. Ice will run communications from inside the truck. Logan will run comm from down here."

Stone looked over to see Logan's flat glare. "Hey, Logan. Glad it's you this time and not me." Stone grinned at the sour look on his friend's face.

Logan had been shot up pretty good not very long ago, and though he was recovering, his muscles hadn't responded as well as they should have. He was doing physiotherapy and rebuilding his strength again, but that didn't mean he couldn't pack a sniper rifle for hours and still make the shots he needed to.

However, Logan was also a whiz with communications, so this was a perfect fit for him.

It also explained why Ice would be in the truck, communicating with Logan and whoever else was running late, which would in this case, be Levi.

Ice also had been injured—her upper arm—so she'd healed faster than Logan. Another sour point in Logan's life. But he was a good guy, and if need be, he'd pick up that rifle and run through the swamp, desert, or forest or jump out of a plane with the rest of them. Given a chance he'd actually beat them all to the other side. They were a small team, only seven of them at the moment, all having finally moved permanently into the Texas compound. Still they'd done plenty in the military with that many men. Levi expected nothing less from them now.

In fact, he expected a lot more because they weren't constrained by the same rules. Although it also meant he didn't have to follow the same regulations. Sometimes those were a good thing. Levi ran a tight ship, and so far they'd all gotten along just fine.

Levi walked over to Stone as he stood staring at the sniper rifles. "You okay, buddy?"

Stone knew what Levi was asking. "I'm fine. We're good to go."

No need to hash out the fact that this was his first active mission since having his leg blown apart. No way in hell was he getting left behind again. You started that; it never ended. He'd be the one staying with Alfred, the one who kept the compound running and the meals cooking. Plus the team needed Stone. They had so much damn work, they were bringing in more men.

The world was in a sad state of affairs.

"Listen up, everyone," Levi said. "We're out in one hour. Stock up on water because it'll get hot as hell out there today."

Damn. Stone hated the heat. But it didn't matter. This was the job. He'd make sure he was up for it one way or another.

LISSA BRAMPTON CROUCHED behind the door, her ear pressed tight against the wood. She could hear spats of conversation, but didn't understand what was being said. She hadn't been over here long enough to pick up any of the language. Although she'd picked up Spanish and French fairly easily while studying it, she wasn't having the same experience with the Afghan tongues.

But their tone wasn't hard to understand. Something was going on. The men were yelling at one another, and she heard sounds of running feet. Thankfully nobody came in her direction.

She looked at the other two hostages. The three of them had been taken from the refugee camp. A husband and wife, both doctors, and her. Somehow they'd been singled out, probably because they were all Americans.

She didn't know if the kidnappers knew who her father was, but it was likely. She understood the rebels had been asking for a lot of money in order to secure her release, but she also knew the American government's policy was to not pay ransoms to terrorists.

In theory she agreed, but now that her head was on the chopping block, not so much.

She stared down at her hands, not surprised when they clenched into fists yet again. It didn't matter that she'd come to this country of her own free will in the first place. She'd defied her father's wishes and left once again as fast as she could. She had volunteered all over the world, and still couldn't be far enough away from her mother and father. He wasn't an easy man to live with, and watching the relationship between her parents was enough to make anybody flee. He would never change. Her mother would always be this frail, clingy listen-to-your-father-type woman.

Thankfully she had her own condo in a different state. She'd left home as soon as she was old enough.

It didn't matter that inside her head was a brain that supposedly functioned on its own. It also didn't matter that her father had wanted a son; instead he'd gotten Lissa. At least she tried not to make it matter. His attitude toward women was less than inspiring. As his daughter, she was supposed to be a clone of her mother. That wasn't working so well. Lissa had more spine than any other woman she knew. Instead of that being a benefit, all it had done was get her in trouble time and time again.

She reached up and checked out the couple of stitches along her temple. It still hurt like shit. Getting stitches without any anesthesia was not something she'd recommend. But she was grateful to Kevin for putting them in. When they'd been kidnapped, Kevin had been packing up several first aid kits, and those, as well as some of their bags, had been grabbed along with them. He'd managed to keep Susan's bag with them initially, and thankfully it had yielded a small first aid kit.

Lissa turned and contemplated the older woman and her husband. They were in their mid- to late-fifties. Having raised their family, they'd wanted to do more with their skills. So they'd headed out and traveled for the last four years, helping out where and how they could.

Somehow they'd ended up here. Now Susan looked tired, worn out.

Lissa's head pounded, and she was desperately in need of water. But ever since they'd been shoved into this room, they'd been given very little, just enough to stay alive. A bucket was in the far corner, which they had tactically agreed to use for waste, and other than that, not a whole lot was here.

She wasn't into whining, but it had been like this for days.

She walked over to the small window too high to climb up, being a good six to eight feet above ground. She could probably do it with help, but no way would she leave anybody behind. This place was a death trap, and she wasn't like her father.

The beam of sunshine shone on her face where she stood. She didn't need the warmth, but something was just so soothing about being in the sunlight.

Even if just a scrap, she badly needed that piece of hope.

Behind her, Susan whispered, "Do you think we'll ever get out of here?"

And Susan was desperately in need of that ray of hope Lissa had found for herself. With as much conviction as she could, Lissa whispered, "Yes. We will. Rest. Build up your strength. We'll have to draw on it."

And she turned to let the sun shine on her face again. If she stood at the right angle, she could see a distant hilltop. The faraway details were blurry.

Something had changed though. She frowned as she studied the horizon. She had had nothing else to look at in the last few days, so she'd memorized the shape of the landscape in her head. Now an extra shadow fell to the left. And then she caught sight of a flash on the hillside. Was that the rebel leader's men up there? Or was someone, even now, searching for them? Maybe there *was* one advantage to being a senator's daughter.

Just as she decided she should sit down and catch a nap, footsteps raced toward them. She didn't have time to decide if she should hide behind the door and attack, or just fall to the ground and pretend to have passed out from lack of water and food. Suddenly two people were already inside the room.

And screaming at them.

Chapter 2

T HE THREE HOSTAGES were grabbed and shoved from the room and down several steps. They were pushed into another room, and the door slammed shut. Not a word was spoken to them; nothing was asked of them.

This room was larger with a door down at the far end; Lissa walked over and opened it. She grinned. She turned to the other two. "It's a bathroom."

Also a hell of a relief because water came from the sink faucet. She walked back into the center of the room to find Kevin standing at the table, then the two women rapidly left.

"They brought us water and food," he said by way of explanation. "Not much of it but enough to keep us alive."

They wanted Susan to eat first as she was in the weakest condition. But Susan wasn't having any of that. She made sure everybody got equal amounts of both, the water and a rice dish of some kind with a little bit of meat and vegetables.

In truth only enough food for one of them. But, like Kevin said, it would keep them alive, which was all that was required at this point. After they ate, Lissa explored the space. It appeared to be identical to what they had had upstairs, but larger.

Still no furniture besides the table, nor blankets or anything to sit on. Just one window, which was slightly bigger than the last.

She took a closer look. They appeared to be on the second floor but still facing the same side of the building. And this time bars were on the windows. Right. No escape that way. But she couldn't help but reach out and give the bars a good shake, just to make sure.

They were solid. And the walls were stone and adobe, traditional native building materials. It would take a grenade or earthquake to make these walls come tumbling down. And considering several floors were above them that would be the worst scenario since they would be flattened inside.

Disgruntled at that concept, she turned to study the rest of the space, but there was nothing more to see. Susan had gone to lie down on the left side of the room, and Kevin held her in his arms. Lissa turned toward the table, but it wouldn't provide much in the way of weaponry either. Simple but old, rickety.

If she were to hit anybody with a piece of it, that would only piss them off, and she'd be in worse shape than ever.

She walked to the door—a big old plank—and studied the hinges. She was surprised this room, like the other, had a door, as mostly just cloth was draped over the openings here. But then this was some kind of a boss's house, and he seemed to expect prisoners here. She reached out and grasped the handle of the door they had been shoved through and pulled it.

Surprise, surprise … The door swung open. Had the serving women not locked it on the way out? Or did the doors not lock?

Instantly two men appeared before her, weapons raised and pointed at her. She held up her hands in apology and pointed to the empty plates on the table. She walked over, grabbed the dishes, held them out, and said, "Please, may we have some more food?"

The two men looked at her with disgust, grabbed them, and left, closing the door tightly behind them. And she somehow knew, even if one had walked away, the other would still be standing guard.

So locks were hardly needed.

Well, she had tried. Just as she decided to lie down also, the door opened again. This time a young girl walked in, carrying a tray with more food. With a smile of thanks, Lissa stepped over to the table and studied the fresh rice and vegetables. More than they had the first time around. Good. Maybe they wouldn't starve yet.

She turned toward Kevin and Susan to see if they wanted any more to eat. Kevin held up his finger to his lips for Lissa to be quiet. She realized Susan had fallen asleep. Also good.

Lissa took a plate with one-third of the food to Kevin. Then she took another for herself. When Susan woke up, some would be there for her to eat. Lissa sat down against the wall across from them and proceeded to fill her tummy. Surprisingly good. But, then again, starvation made anything taste good.

When she finished, she placed her plate on the table and returned to her spot on the floor. It would get cold when night came. But she didn't think blankets would be offered. She'd been cold before, and it was preferable than being hungry.

Feeling a whole lot better, she curled up like Susan and slept.

STONE STUDIED THE layout of the compound below him. He was surprised when they found places like this—a complete oasis compared to the rest of the village on the other side.

Some wealthy man had decided to build himself quite the place here. Large enough to hold an entire village comfortably—nobody would even have to share space, from what Stone could see. Also several good-size trucks drove around, moving inventory from one side of the compound to the other. Stone presumed weapons, considering they needed trucks to move them.

With his scope, Stone estimated the distance to the outside wall to be four hundred yards. Another ten to the inside wall of the actual building. He slowly assessed any weaknesses. His gaze landed on the second-story window, worried about the young woman he'd seen before. She'd been there for a brief moment and then was gone. Now he wondered who she was. But, as she'd been the only blonde he'd seen since they had arrived in this damn country, it was a safe bet that was Lissa Brampton. Intel had said she was here. He was inclined to believe it now.

He had been on enough missions where the data had been wrong so he never trusted it until he could confirm the same with his own eyes. What he didn't like was the wind picking up. That made for shitty shots. Not impossible but it just added to the complexity.

A lot of people were in the compound. His team needed to make a diversion, then sneak in for the hostages, and get the hell out of here. The diversion was Levi's job on the far side. All seven members of the team were here, but with only four on the ground, that didn't allow for a lot of cover. Ice was controlling something inside the vehicle that gave them a hell of an advantage though—one of Bullard's new drones.

Those things were something else. The military used them to pick off known terrorist members one at a time all over the world. They were deadly accurate. Stone crept toward the truck where Ice stood. She had two drones set up. It helped that she was the helicopter pilot from hell or maybe she just happened to have a natural aptitude to take to these drones like a boss man. None of the others had the same fine-tuned control she did with them.

"Are you ready?"

She nodded. "Bullard sent instructions on how to muffle the noise ever-so-slightly." She reached down and adjusted something in the rear of the small machine. "Just finished tinkering with it." She glanced at Stone. "Anything from Levi?"

He shook his head. "Not yet."

And all that changed two minutes later.

Ice sent both drones in the sky, directing them around back where Levi was setting up charges on the far side of the wall, hoping the blast would lure everybody over, giving Rhodes and Merk a chance to make their move while Stone and Harrison covered their backs.

Ice tensed beside Stone, watching the screens and controlling two drones at once. She carefully picked off the men on the outside, away from the action.

Stone looked at her with respect. "Two already?" he asked.

She didn't take her eyes off the screens. "Yes."

Then Levi's charges blew. The compound erupted.

The drones were a matte black and, like a bat in the night, were very hard to see until they moved. Plus they hovered at a very unique speed, making them difficult to pinpoint in the night sky.

"Five," she said in a cool tone.

Stone grinned. Maybe he didn't need a sniper rifle after all. He was ready and lined up, but saw no targets. Then he stiffened.

Rhodes and Merk appeared suddenly. With all the gunfire and explosions on the far side, the two of them had scrambled to the side. How did they know where the girl was? But they headed for the blonde he'd seen earlier. Very quickly they had lines thrown up and caught in the bars, and they scaled the wall. Damn, they were good. Something he wasn't sure he'd ever be able to do with his leg now. Well, maybe he could, just not as fast.

He peered through his scope. Harrison scouted the bottom area. Suddenly the bars in the window blew apart, and both men went inside. In Stone's mind, he urged, *Go, go, go.*

The two men disappeared into the room beyond them, then they came out with the blonde and a second woman.

Shit, they weren't expecting a second hostage. When Rhodes and Merk repeated the climb and exited with a man between them, Stone knew things would be a whole lot more difficult than he had originally thought. It was one thing for them to pick up and carry a single woman, but it was another for two men to handle three people.

Just as Rhodes and Merk lowered the rescued guy to the ground, an unfriendly came around the corner. His head exploded even as Stone readied his shot. Damn it. Harrison got him.

There. Stone pulled the trigger, and the second man went down. After that, pick and shoot, pick and shoot.

He kept track of Merk and Rhodes and the hostages' progress but just barely. He could hear Ice swearing behind him and knew she was still at work. A funny poof in the sky went off to the left. He watched as one of the drones blew up. Behind him, Ice said, "Shit."

Hell, he didn't know what she expected. That damn thing had taken out twice as many people as he had, and he was damn good.

His earpiece crackled. "Retreat."

Easy for Levi to say. They now had a total of ten people to extract from this nightmare. Leaving Harrison to give the others cover, Stone and Ice bailed into the same truck. He started the engine to soon be able to gather the hostages. In the darkness he crept down the hill, doing his damnedest to avoid the rocks and trees he'd scoped out earlier.

Almost to the bottom, Merk moved to meet the double-cab truck. Stone picked up a sniper rifle and took several cover shots as the hostages were loaded inside the rear cab. They were parked at a shitty angle, and they still had Levi to find and Harrison to collect. Logan would drive the lead truck, pick up Merk and Rhodes, and then meet up with them soon.

"Drive, Stone," Ice snapped. "I'll take them down."

He transferred the rifle to her. She sat on the open window, firing over the hood of the truck. He drove the vehicle backward and around onto the road and then hightailed it out of there.

Yelling, he asked, "Where's Harrison?"

"He's coming, twenty yards in front of us." She looked around and added, "But where the hell is Levi?"

Stone had no idea.

That happened when people made plans.

They went to shit. Always.

He hit the gas and drove as fast as he could to pick up Harrison. Stone knew Levi. He'd be here when they least expected him.

Harrison jumped on the running board behind Ice as Stone gunned it. He could feel the tension from everybody in the vehicle. Nobody in the back said a word. Ice never did, but he knew damn well what was on her mind. Levi had to be here somewhere.

They wrapped around the mountain they'd been climbing and headed toward the village. They no longer had a safe place for them. In fact, from the looks of the dust curling up the hillside behind them, they were about to have unwelcome visitors.

Ice opened up the laptop for the minefield software. "I'll navigate. You drive."

His earpiece crackled. "Stone, keep coming. I'm ten yards to the right. Stop and I'll jump on."

Stone had barely hit the brakes when he felt Levi leap into the pickup bed.

Harrison joined him there, yelling at Stone, "Unfriendlies on our ass. Move!"

Stone hit the gas, hating the thought of finding his way at top speeds in the dark.

"Don't worry about it. I got this." Ice barked orders that barely had time to register as she sent them right, then left and right, and left again and now straight forward.

By the time they finally made it to the other side, Stone's adrenaline was running at top speed. A pickup point was ahead, and a vehicle change needed to happen damn fast. Stone hadn't been able to shake the rebels on their ass. In fact, it looked like they'd been following his tail all the way out.

"We've got another minefield ahead," Ice said. "If we do this correctly, we can take them out at the same time. Take a left now."

Instantly he jerked the truck, hearing a soft gasp from behind him. He ignored it.

"And a right ... *now*." Again he jerked the wheel and a land mine went off just behind him.

He glanced at Ice. "That was too close."

She shrugged and grinned at him in the dark. "It was necessary."

He raised his eyebrows but kept on driving until he heard a huge *boom*. Glancing in his rearview mirror, he watched as the truck following them hit a mine full-on. The vehicle was blasted into the air and tumbled before blowing up.

Beside him, Ice closed the laptop and said, "Good job."

Stone laughed. "You mean, *damn* good job."

"Are you people nuts?"

The soft female voice from behind him was the first of the hostages to talk. Stone really hadn't been aware of their presence. What must they have thought of this last hour of panic? He shook his head. Maybe he was crazy, but they'd been smart enough to listen to him and stay quiet. He could appreciate that.

He twisted and gave a quick glance behind him. "You guys okay?" He returned his gaze to the road and asked a second question. "Anybody need medical help?"

"No. Kevin and Susan are doctors themselves," the blonde said. "They're just tired. I'm fine too."

Ice turned to study her. "Melissa Brampton?"

The young woman nodded. "Yes, I'm Lissa."

"Good. Your father's waiting at home for you."

"He actually paid the ransom?"

The shock in her voice made Stone send another quick glance her way in the rearview mirror. She did appear to be in a daze. Whether in shock from the recent events or at the thought that her father might care enough to pay, he wasn't sure.

He decided he'd take one of those doubts out of the question. "Yes, he was quite prepared to pay the ransom. However, the decision was made to come in and rescue you because paying did not guarantee your life."

She nodded silently. "That's what I figured. Never thought he would pay though."

Her words had a slight tone of bitterness that made him and Ice exchange a look.

Then the blonde added, "He was never one to back a losing horse."

Stone didn't know what the hell that meant, but obviously there was some strain in the relationship between father and daughter. Although events like this tended to make even the worst relationships a whole lot better. He wasn't so sure that was the case this time though.

In the rearview mirror he took a long look at her for the first time and was surprised by what he saw. For a woman who had defied her father to come to do good works in a country on the far side of the Earth, a war-torn country at that, he'd expected somebody strong, robust even. Instead she sat tall and lean. Maybe there was a strength to her, but he saw only fragility instead.

What was likely very fair blonde hair under all that grime had been tied in a braid. Her face was covered in dirt, her clothes torn, and she looked like she had just survived a heart-wrenching ordeal. Which, in fact, she had. Yet he could see the strength in her face and her gaze, but physically she was the exact opposite of what he had pictured.

He also wasn't expecting the sucker punch to his gut. Then again he wasn't into showpieces. He liked women with grit, and she appeared to have it, in spades.

Ice's hand whacked him across his arm, making him realize his mind had wandered again. He turned his gaze forward and kept his focus on the road. The last thing he needed was to be sidelined by a woman, full of grit or not.

"Well, he did," Ice snapped in response to Lissa's last two comments. "Although there's no way in hell our team would be looked upon as a losing horse."

Chapter 3

LISSA DIDN'T KNOW the woman in the front seat of the vehicle. But she was obviously in charge and capable. A part of Lissa felt like she should rebel against that authority; another part told her to just shut up, sit back, and relax. She didn't have to be in control all the time. And she needed to learn to let go more. It seemed like she'd been on the warpath her whole life, ever since she had been old enough to understand that she didn't want to do or follow every dictate sent her way.

Besides, these people had come to rescue her. And had done an admirable job of it so far. She understood they were likely very highly paid for the job, but still she appreciated them. Their lives were in just as much danger as her own at this point.

She closed her eyes and got settled, giving in. With a calm voice she said, "I meant no offense to your team, simply that my father considered *me* to be a losing horse. But my relationship with him is not in question here."

The driver, a huge beef of a man, spoke up quietly. "Ice is just very protective of us. This is what we do."

"And you did it wonderfully. I thank you for saving me," she said without opening her eyes. "I'm just too tired right now to even think straight."

Kevin reached across the backseat and gently patted Lissa

on the shoulder. "We're all very grateful for what you've done. I wasn't sure how much longer my wife would last, to be honest," he admitted. "It's been a tough couple years, but this last week was by far the worst. Of course the kidnapping was the highlight."

Ice turned to stare at them from the front seat. "Week?"

He nodded. "The disruptions at the refugee camp seemed to be getting much worse every day. In fact, we should've known something like this was bound to happen. Not that there were signs, but ... there *were*. You know?"

"Right—the men watching, the extra military weapons showing up, just the ratcheted-up level of fear and tension around the place," Stone said.

Lissa nodded and agreed with him 100 percent. "If we had been smart enough, we would've understood what was going on and left a week ago. Even a few days before would've been lovely." Her lips twisted in a half-sad smile. "Instead we got pulled into this mess. Something I could've done without."

"All three of us could have missed this *opportunity*," Kevin said with a smile. "On the other hand, thanks to your people, we have survived." He glanced outside the windows of the truck and said, "We *are* out of danger now, aren't we?"

"We're never fully out of it," Ice said. "But with every mile we put between them and us, we will be better off."

"We're about an hour away from the vehicle transfer, so just sit back and relax," Stone said. "We'll keep watch."

Lissa turned and looked through the glass windows behind them. "What about the two men in the truck bed? Are they okay?"

"They will be. We're actually meeting another truck up ahead. We'll be shuffling men at that point."

And, about an hour later, Lissa watched as this vehicle then slowed and pulled up beside an older pickup with a man leaning against it, as if waiting for them. Once their truck stopped, the door opened. The man took a look at the backseat and raised his eyebrows. "Three hostages? Are they doing okay?"

Ice nodded. "How are Merk and Rhodes holding up?"

Lissa looked around and realized that the two men who had hauled her from that room weren't actually in the truck she rode in. But she could see them now in the other vehicle. Oh, thank God. As they watched and waited, one of the men in the rear of her pickup hopped out. She only half listened as plans were made.

The last man from the pickup bed came around to the front. She didn't know where these men were born and bred but they were seriously badass-looking dudes. And something about that right now made her feel damn comfortable. It was nice to think she was safe for a change. It seemed like she hadn't felt that way for a long time, if ever in her life.

While she pondered the comparison, the big man got into the front seat with Ice and the driver, who she thought somebody had called Stone. In a way that fit. He had to weigh 250 pounds easy. If not fifty more than that.

She had felt like a Chihuahua, wanting to snap at the Dobermans, the rebels, telling them to keep away. But compared to them, these men were bloody Newfoundlanders, outweighing and outgunning them. She only hoped they were meaner than their dog counterpart.

Being raised by her father with his own Doberman mentality always nipping away at her self-confidence had made her very wary of other men.

Stone turned around to look at her. "Lissa, how are you

doing?"

Just enough real interest in his voice and his gaze had her realizing, even though this might be a job, he was concerned.

She smiled up at him, her first genuine smile in a while, and said, "I'm doing fine, thanks. I'm just so glad to be safe."

He nodded in understanding. "You're still not fully safe yet," he cautioned. "Not until we get you home on American soil."

"Understood." She watched as his gaze traveled to the other two former hostages, a frown developing as he studied Susan. He twisted in his seat to look at Susan's husband.

Kevin said with a smile, "She's just exhausted. We're both doctors, and have been burning the midnight oil for a long time."

Only the big man didn't appear to be appeased. "I know who Lissa is, but I do need to know your names. And nationality."

"Kevin and Susan Salinger, both Americans, born in Kansas. After we became empty-nesters, we decided to find a new purpose in life." With a lopsided smile he said, "Maybe it's time to go home."

"This is Levi and Ice, and I'm your driver, Stone. I'd tell you the names of the other four men in the second truck, but you'll forget and won't have a face to put with them, so we'll do those introductions later. We were actually hired by Lissa's father to bring her home, and you just happened to be in the right place at the right time."

Kevin gave a bark of laughter at that. "While that's a hell of an insight, it's better than being in the wrong place at the wrong time, which is how we felt. We were kidnapped with Lissa." He reached up a hand to shake Levi's and said, "Thank you for being kind enough to pick up two extra people in need."

"No problem and no charge. We're all former US Navy, and this is what we've always done. Now we just do it privately."

He turned around to sit back, facing the front, adding, "There's another stop in about forty-five minutes. We'll grab a bite to eat, take a bathroom break, and switch vehicles. Expect to leave on a flight in six hours, if all goes according to plan."

Lissa really wished he hadn't said the last part but understood his need to clarify. She knew it would be a hell of a long journey; they just had to be patient. She was rather desperate to get home now, but it didn't really matter how much time it took to get there—as long as they escaped from this hellhole.

STONE DROVE STEADILY through the darkness. Even though the mission was a success so far, this was not the time to let down his guard. Too many missions went off the rails because people thought they were safe. He and his team weren't at that point yet.

According to his calculations they were about five minutes out from the rendezvous. He drove onto the side street in front of the large warehouse building and parked, shutting off the lights. There was absolute silence inside the vehicle.

The other half of the team had driven past the warehouse and entered from the far side. One of the rules was to never be in the same place at the same time. Too easy for them all to get taken out. But they had to be close enough to back each other up in case something went wrong.

He glanced at Levi and raised an eyebrow. Even in the half-light he could see Levi's frown.

They waited. Two new vehicles were supposedly standing by for them. Stone checked his watch and realized they were actually two minutes early.

The earphone crackled in his ear. "No activity on the site."

"Silent here."

And they waited.

And waited. At five minutes past the appointed hour, Levi opened the door and slipped out. Ice followed. Stone pulled his handgun free of his holster and laid it on the seat beside him. With those two checking things out, it would be just him and three hostages. Not good odds.

He quickly relayed the change of status to the rest of the team. Better to be safe than sorry.

He could feel the hostages behind him shuffling, looking around, the tension building inside the truck. In as calm a voice as he could, he said, "Nobody else has shown up for the rendezvous. Levi and Ice have gone to check it out."

"And you're expecting trouble, I presume," Lissa said.

"I'm always expecting trouble."

Kevin murmured, "That must be a tough way to live."

Stone shrugged. "I spent a lot of years in the military as part of an elite team doing missions all around the world. Waiting, ready to go in at a moment's notice. From the time we were called up, it was like this every minute until we were home safe and sound." His gaze never stopped wandering, checking the area outside the vehicle. He wanted to go in and search, but no way would he leave these people here. But he didn't trust this situation. When things went wrong, they went really wrong in his world. Quietly he ordered, "Hunker down."

He quickly ducked below the dashboard.

And they waited. His communication bud crackled again. "One stranger on the left. We're on your right coming up against the side of the truck."

"Understood." He stayed where he was and waited. When shots rang out, he snapped to the people in the backseat, "Stay down."

He crawled out on Levi's side of the truck. Harrison was behind him, on the tailgate. Stone crept forward to peer around.

A second gunshot fired. And then that ever-waiting stillness that came after. Was there another shooter? And who was actually doing the shooting? Merk or someone else? His earpiece crackled. "All clear. One down."

Good.

Except for one thing. Unfriendlies never came alone— they were always with friends.

And this time was no different.

Chapter 4

LISSA CLASPED HER hands over her ears and pinched her lips together to keep the cry of fear from squeaking out. After all they'd been through, she'd hoped to be free of this torment. Instead they were apparently caught up in some other bit of nastiness. The war in Afghanistan had very long-reaching tentacles. She had no idea who was after whom. She prided herself on staying away from politics. Anything in that direction reminded her of her father. She wasn't a child of the sixties and didn't have that whole flower-power thing going on, but she certainly believed in a fair wage for all and wanted to promote peace, not war. She had a hard time with a lot of the political stands taken in her own country right now.

With the presidential election, everything was topsy-turvy. She just wanted the people to get their heads out of the ground and realize something needed to happen to promote the family unit, keep the peace, and do something to help each other. Whatever happened to honesty, ethics, and morals? It seemed like all that had gone by the wayside.

Even manners, such a basic building block of society, were gone. That was partly why she'd been so disillusioned and had allowed her father's final words to send her off—again—overseas. She'd just run out of faith in mankind. And that was hardly fair because a lot of good people were out there. She had met many while doing volunteer work. But there was just something about being in her father's stuffy old house with the windows closed and the maids who never said a word, always silent, always watching. She wondered if they were laughing at her. She didn't even know if they spoke English. Her father was fluent in Spanish, and she wondered if he even paid them a fair wage. She had a hard time with all of it. But at the same time, she knew the maids needed the money to send back home.

Instead of being a win-win situation, to her it was lose-lose on both ends. But there was really no good answer. Frustrated, feeling incapable of changing anything, she'd taken off to the areas she understood.

People who were still focused on the basics of life. Who toiled in the fields all day and broke bread happily as a family at night. Whose only entertainment was storytelling, making simple things with their hands, singing, and dancing. It had been joyous to experience.

She closed her eyes and tried to relax as the men tracked down the rest of their team. She could only hope nobody else would be hurt because of her actions. Her father was right about that. If she hadn't run to help with the refugee camp, nobody would've come after her, putting their own lives in danger. It didn't matter if they were paid or did this on a regular basis. If one of them died, she'd feel terrible.

Way too late for recriminations now. She knew somebody had been shot out there; she just hoped it wasn't one of the rescue team.

On the other hand, if it was one of the enemy, how many more were there?

Susan's tired voice startled her in the silent truck. "What's going on? Where are we?"

She could hear Kevin's low murmur as he tried to comfort his wife. His explanation was done in soft tones, as if that would matter.

The harshness of the scenario had Lissa wanting to run from the truck and do something. Being confined was killing her soul, and bringing up her fear. She used to have panic attacks all the time growing up. But she could lay the blame for that at her father's feet. They began after he locked her in the closet when she wasn't "being good." She thought she had overcome her confined-space issue when she'd finally taken the elevators instead of escalators. It had taken her a long time and a lot of tears and sleepless nights to get to the point where she could now ride them freely. But that didn't mean she liked them.

And now she was in this truck. And although not confined in the same sense of the word, it felt restricting and, even if she left, she had no place to go. She tried to control her breathing, but the panic was setting in. She closed her eyes, clenched her fists, and took great big gulping breaths, but it wasn't enough.

Finally she couldn't stand it. She bolted upright and rolled onto the front seat to push open the passenger door, leaning out, taking in large amounts of fresh air. Behind her she could hear Kevin's shocked gasp. But she couldn't worry about that. She was too busy sucking in oxygen.

As she held the door, the tremors working down her arm made it shake in the night. A strong hand reached up to grip her arm. She didn't know if it was to hold her in place to stop the shaking, or to make her relinquish her hold on the door. No success with the latter. Instead she gripped it like a lifeline.

She didn't have time to react as a face appeared in the

darkness. Instead of being scared, she was relieved to identify Stone, their driver.

He studied her with concern. "You okay?"

She nodded barely. "I just ... I just needed fresh air."

But she could tell from the intensity of his gaze that he knew there was more to it. Now that she was no longer alone, and fresh air swooped through the place, she started to relax. She took several more deep breaths, telling her body to calm down, that it would be okay.

When he lifted her hand off the doorframe, she let him. But when he slid his down to hold hers, she froze.

Gently he squeezed her fingers together, a rough thumb stroking up and down on the back of her fingers. "It's okay. Being scared is a normal reaction. You've been through a lot already."

If he only knew. She gave him a slight smile and added, "I could've managed all that. But when you left me locked up in the truck ..." She shook her head. "I thought I'd been doing so much better lately, but sometimes being confined gets to me."

He smiled and patted her hand. "I can leave the door slightly ajar if that makes it better, but I can't just stay here."

She tensed at the thought that he was leaving.

Instantly he squeezed her fingers and said, "Don't worry. I'm staying at the side of the vehicle. I'm not leaving you. It's my job to stand guard here."

"My hero," she said with a light groan. But, of course, it was his job. Still it didn't matter; she was such a mess right now she was grateful for anyone's support. She lowered her head to her other arm and just relaxed across the front seat. Her hand was still in his as he gently reassured her that she would be okay.

She thought she was out of the worst of the danger, and it was safe to relax. Then she heard a shout in the distance. Lifting her head, she studied Stone. "What is that?"

He lifted her palm to his lips and dropped a gentle kiss on the back of her hand and said, "Don't worry. It's one of my men, not the enemy."

In the distance she heard, "Stone?"

Instantly he straightened. He ducked down to look at her and said, "Stay here. I'll be back in two minutes."

She snorted. As if she was going anywhere. No way in hell. She was warm, safe, and dry. And soon this vehicle would get her the hell out of here. But none of that made her feel any better right now.

She pulled her hand in and tucked it against her chest, wondering at his gentle kiss. For such a huge man, the graceful gesture of comfort seemed out of place—and yet not. His actions had been smooth, natural. And that made all the difference.

With her arms tucked up close, she huddled in the front, listening for the men to come back. Only they didn't come anytime soon.

And her return home was to be delayed yet again. She rolled to her back and stared straight up at the ceiling. A chill set in. Likely shock. "Kevin, you doing okay?"

"Susan's asleep again. We're both fine."

But she could hear the underlying worry in his voice. They were all fine. But for how long?

STONE RACED TOWARD the other men, wondering what the hell had gotten into him. Since when did he ever kiss a woman's hand like she was some kind of royalty? It was so not him. But at the time, it seemed to be the best thing to do.

He'd understood the panic attack. Hell, the signs were damn-near impossible to miss. She gulped the air like she was dying. Anything that would help her stay calm and inside was a good thing. He just tossed it off as a casual gesture to make her feel better. Yet he knew it had to be a little bit more than that.

He wasn't sure what the attraction was, but just watching her struggle to control herself added to the admiration he felt already. She hadn't bolted. She'd only opened the truck door enough to get fresh air in. She could have opened the window.

And then he thought about that and stopped, saying to himself, "No, she couldn't have. They were power windows, and I didn't leave the keys in the ignition. So she did what she could."

Smart. He liked that. But not her hero comment. Still he'd take it as a joke as he had no intention of being called a hero. He'd been tagged with that label once too often—relationships where people looked up to him, seeing him as something he wasn't, only to find out he had feet of clay.

Besides he wasn't who he had been anymore either. He was no fool, and that was a fact. Missing a leg was very hard to ignore. He didn't know if Lissa had even noticed, and didn't want to see the look on her face when she finally did. He'd seen a few women's expressions already. Most had been decent about it, but some had twisted their features with revulsion. That had been more than enough for him.

He approached the body on the ground and bent down to take a pulse. Nothing. He glanced at Harrison. "Did you shoot him?"

Harrison nodded and held up another weapon in his hand. "He came up behind me with the gun to my back."

"Right." Stone looked down at the rebel on the ground. "We need to move his body. Anyone can see him here." He glanced around. "Are there others?"

Harrison shook his head. "We've done a full sweep. Levi is talking with Logan right now. We're running behind."

Just as Harrison finished speaking, Levi raced toward them. "We need to move it."

Stone motioned to the body on the ground. "What do we do with him?"

Levi didn't break a sweat as he said, "Leave him there. If we move him, it'll look more suspicious. At this point, I have to say, it's not our problem."

Stone was delighted to find Lissa sitting in the backseat again, staring out the window. He caught her glance and smiled at her encouragingly as he started the engine and turned the vehicle around.

"No vehicle exchange?" she asked quietly.

Levi answered, "No. Change of plans."

"But we'll still make the airport?"

"We'll make it. Don't know if we'll make it in time for your flight though."

Stone watched as she slid lower into the back corner. From the rearview mirror he had a perfect angle to see her as she settled in. With her arms wrapped around her chest and her head resting against the door, it looked like she would try to nap. He highly approved. She'd been running on empty for a long time. Her face was gaunt—he'd felt the bones inside her fingers; the skin over the top of them was sheer, thin. Except for the few calluses where she'd obviously been working hard lately. Overall nothing to take away from the fact that she was very well put together.

But he damn well better keep his mind on the job at hand, not on the curves he could barely see—but had no trouble imagining.

The roads were empty. He drove like crazy to get to the airport on time. When he pulled in, a small plane awaited them, the pilot impatiently stamping his feet at the stairs. Conrad, another friend of Levi's, had been doing flights for them around Europe at odd times. This day he was to take them to London.

"There you are. Finally," he called. "I don't want to have to file another change of flight plan, so let's move it. I've got the paperwork on board." He opened the truck door, motioned them to get out. "Let's go. Let's go. *Let's go.*"

Stone hopped out the driver side and opened the passenger door behind him. Susan, barely awake, was helped to stand up by her husband. But no way could she move very quickly. Nor her husband. Before Stone could make any kind of comment, Levi came around the front of the truck and assessed the situation. He stepped forward quickly, scooping Susan in his arms.

Levi told Kevin, "Come on. Let's go."

Stone checked to see how Lissa was doing. She walked beside them, valiant but tired.

The second truck pulled up beside them, the men getting out and doing a fast sweep. Everyone boarded the plane except for two agents approaching from the small hanger.

Rhodes met the men now responsible for returning the vehicles to the rendezvous point.

Shit went wrong all the time. They had to think on their feet. Plans changed as needed. They were used to it. Inside the plane Stone sat down across from Lissa. This was definitely a no-frills flight. But they would be in London in a few hours. She just needed to hold on a little bit longer.

Levi tucked Susan up against a window seat, and Kevin sat down beside her. They'd barely had a chance to buckle up when Rhodes dashed in to grab his seat.

And the plane began taxiing.

Good. The sooner, the better. Stone watched as the two vehicles they'd driven pulled away, heading back the way they'd come. Now it was just them.

As he looked out the window, it was pitch-black around them. The hangar had no lights and neither did the runway. He shook his head. Typical.

But he also knew Conrad. That man could fly anything anywhere. Just like Ice and her helicopter. Conrad laughed at something Ice said. The two of them were best friends. And at this point, they needed the best they could have. They still weren't out of danger.

Just a few more hours would be good. Stone gazed around the interior of the plane and realized Susan was once again asleep. He studied the color of her face and realized her sleek skin wasn't natural looking. Something was definitely wrong with her. They needed to get her medical attention—and fast. He frowned.

Why hadn't her husband said anything? Did he not know? Was he so stressed that he believed she was just exhausted? Or did he know something more serious was going on but also knew how little anyone could do about it now?

Chapter 5

LONDON? NOW SHE'D finally traveled to a place she'd always wanted to go, but somehow hadn't reached yet. Of course that was again due to her father. She had really wanted to go to school here, but he'd vetoed it, sending her to a private school in the same state where he lived. He had more control over her there. His donations made a difference and also ensured somebody watched her with a close eye. She'd hated him for that.

The other girls in the school thought it was hilarious. They regularly got her into trouble. Still she had been given some freedom, and her father had left her alone while there. But that watchdog presence had hovered over her future until she could get away.

London was a reminder of the constant battle between her and her father. Only as an adult did she finally break free. When she moved out on her own, she thought he would have a heart attack. Somehow in his mind, she would stay at home until he found the right husband for her.

He'd been introducing her to men for a long time. But they were all his cronies, older men looking for trophy wives. She'd heard her father actually refer to her as a potential up-and-coming one. It made her stomach curdle. She was anything but. As her father had often said, *She looks pretty, but she has a bite. You'll need to control her with a firm hand.*

Was there ever a statement that would send this potential trophy wife screaming in the opposite direction? A firm hand? Yeah, not what she wanted.

She stared out at the huge city below. The bright lights were a godsend. They meant safety to her. They landed, disembarked, and cleared customs at Heathrow with relative ease. Levi had large packets of documentation, and their gun cases were even allowed in. She wondered how many people actually got weapons through high-security places like this. These men had ways and means of accomplishing things she'd never seen.

She walked beside Stone. Since he got on the plane, he hadn't said a word. Just like his namesake, he'd sat there, rigid and unbending. Every once in a while, she watched him massage his left leg. And she wondered if it was an old injury. He was a big man. That body had to be taking a hell of a brutal beating with these kinds of missions. She was sorry if she had added any stress or pain to his life.

She was tall and appreciated tall men. The guy was built like a square tank. She was fairly slim, and this guy would make two of her easily. Still there was something very attractive about that strong silent type. Although, if he would crack a smile every once in a while, she'd appreciate it.

He was quite the protective bulldog at her side. They were catching some attention as they walked as a group. Mostly everybody stepped out of their path to avoid them. Ice and Levi as a couple were very striking, but dressed as they were, it was hardly a relationship-type look for them. All the men of this team were big, fit, and looked ready for any kind of trouble.

The busy airport was suddenly free and clear for them to walk through. She giggled at the thought. She could really use these guys when shopping at the malls.

Stone looked her way, and in a low voice, he asked, "What's so funny?"

She smiled at him. "I was just thinking how helpful it would be to have you guys go shopping with me in the malls. Pathways magically appear when you are around."

His gaze narrowed as he studied the airport, and then his lips quirked. "Not everyone's stupid. They can see danger when it's coming at them."

At that she laughed out loud. "Hell, fear is a big motivating factor for everyone."

He shrugged. "They don't have anything to be afraid of from me."

She shot him a look of straight disbelief. "Surely you are not unaware of how you present yourself. Most people would run away screaming if they were to happen upon you accidentally in the dark."

He frowned and said shortly, "Garbage." He spread his huge mitts and added, "I'm a nice guy. No one needs to be afraid of me."

At that she burst into gales of laughter. The others twisted to look at what the two of them were talking about. She caught sight of Stone as he shrugged his massive shoulders as if to say, *She's just having a moment, so ignore her.* She couldn't stop giggling.

She hooked her arm through his and whispered conspiratorially, "You are scary."

He slanted a gaze her way and said, "You don't appear to be afraid of me."

She patted his forearm and snickered. "That's because I'm not. You're just a gentle giant."

Harrison, who'd been walking on the other side of her,

sniggered. "Oh, that's good. We'll just change your name from Stone to Gentle Giant. No problem," he said. "I totally agree."

"See? Even the guys are on my side on this one." And she snickered again.

She knew Stone didn't know what to make of her. So few big men really understood the impression they gave to others. In his case, he probably thought he was harmless. Unless he was in action. Then that man was all devil. On the other hand, he was on her side, so she had no complaints. He had done a kick-ass job of protecting her so far.

They walked down toward the exit doors. A large group of schoolgirls approached and giggled as they went past. Several were flirting with him. She leaned closer and said, "Ya see? They all want a gentle giant of their own to cuddle up to."

Harrison sniggered again, and she was surprised to see a hint of pink wash up Stone's neck and cheeks. He was embarrassed. How absolutely adorable. She patted his forearm, still holding his arm linked with hers and said, "Don't worry. I'll protect you."

His voice low, he said, "You're having way too much fun with this." He walked faster, with Lissa almost skipping beside him.

It made her feel like a schoolgirl herself as she raced to keep up. "My life's been a bit in the dumps for quite a while. Just a little lighthearted humor to put things in perspective."

He shook his head. "You have a strange outlook on life."

She laughed. "I know you don't appreciate my negativity against my father, but you really have to meet the man."

"What did he do that made you so upset?"

"Well, he locked me in the closet every time he got mad

at me so I now hate confining spaces. Of course you already know about that. How about the fact that he was lining up suitors for the up-and-coming trophy wife who would need a firm hand because she didn't yet have the right attitude?" She couldn't keep the bitterness from her tone.

He straightened and stared down at her in shock. "You serious?"

She nodded. "Every time I came home from college, he always had a new one ready. And the summer before I moved out, he had one coming in every day for a week. Same introductory line every time. I wasn't sure if a bride-price or dowry would be exchanged. My father likes money so maybe a dowry." She studied Stone's face, noting the muscle flicking in the corner of his jaw. "See? Like I said, he's not exactly an angel."

"He is a senator," Stone said cautiously.

"Yep, he is. For eighteen years now. Hopefully he's doing something good for his constituency because his family certainly suffered." Then she gave a mental shrug. "It doesn't matter. It was a long time ago. I walked away and stayed away. I communicate with him and speak with my mom every once in a while. But I don't have a whole lot to do with either of them." She sighed. "Although I owe him my thanks for sending you guys after me."

"When was the last time you went home?"

"Four years ago for Christmas. I was supposed to stay for four days," she said calmly. "I left the same day."

"More suitors?"

"More suitors, even older ones."

"And just how old are we talking?" he asked in a dangerously quiet voice.

"The last two were in their mid-sixties. My father actually thought I should be grateful because then I'd be a widow before too long. With money and freedom to do as I wanted."

"Sounds like a real prize."

"Yeah. I guess some people would call it that."

They walked out into the fresh air. Rain drizzled, soaking through their clothing to their skin. Of course. They were in London.

"Where are we going now?" she asked Stone.

Levi turned to look at her and answered, "To a house for the night, and we'll fly to the States in the morning."

She nodded. Inside her, relief swelled. She wasn't against going home, but she *was* damn tired. Now that they'd made it this far, the pressure was off. "Sounds good to me, especially if this house has hot running water for a shower," she said with a bit of a smile.

"There are showers for everyone."

They gathered inside a large taxi, heading out of the city within minutes. The cab was barely large enough for half of them, since all the men were Stone's size—maybe not that large, but they were certainly big men. Still they squeezed in, and that was what counted.

She tried to settle in the seat, but was pinned between Harrison and Stone—a large thigh on both sides. "God, you guys are like tanks."

Stone tried to move over, but he had no place to go.

She shrugged and said, "Don't worry about it. I'll be fine."

The trip to the house took twenty minutes. By the time they bailed out, she was feeling the effect of all the travel. It was hard even to look around and be excited about where she was. Just a surreal atmosphere to the whole thing.

As much as she'd wanted to keep reminding herself she was safe, she seemed to be more focused on Stone than anything. He was fascinating. Irritating. And yet very comforting. She somehow latched onto him versus any of the others. She didn't know why; maybe because he was the biggest. Maybe she figured he would offer her the best protection.

Of course it was stupid. She did need protection, but with so many men, she doubted anyone could get through. Levi led them up to a brownstone where he gave the door several raps. The door opened almost instantly. The man who stood there was of the same ilk. She recognized a military bearing, but this one was older. She guessed maybe mid-sixties.

They were all ushered inside where jackets and shoes were taken off, and they were led through to the living room. She had never been in one of these townhouses. She looked around curiously. It was sparse but welcoming. With so many of them, they pretty well filled all available seating. The older man motioned to Kevin and Susan first. "Follow me. I'll take you to your room, and you can get settled for the night."

Kevin stood up. "Thank you very much." He turned to Susan. "Come on, honey. Let's get you up to bed."

She gave him a wan smile and allowed him to help her to her feet once again. She even climbed a few steps on the stairway. Lissa winced. Every step looked to be so damn painful. She wanted to ask if one of the men could help Susan but wasn't sure if that was appropriate.

Kevin was slightly older and also suffering the ill effects of their kidnapping, Levi walked over and said something to Kevin.

With a nod, Kevin stepped back and let Levi help Susan. He easily picked her up, ignoring her weak protests, and quickly climbed the stairs, following their host.

As they disappeared from sight, Lissa turned around to see the others staring at her. "What?"

"Is there something seriously wrong with Susan that we don't know about?" Ice asked.

"I'm not sure," Lissa said. "She's always appeared strong and capable until the kidnapping. I don't know if she has a condition that has suddenly taken a downturn or if it's just exhaustion and shock."

"That could be all it is," Ice said. "She's been through a lot."

That seemed to appease everyone, at least for the moment. Their host returned and cast his gaze around the room, smiling at the various men. And stopped, his gaze landing on her. He walked forward and said, "Hi, I'm Charles. And you are?"

Suddenly nervous, she stood up and shook his hand. "My name is Lissa Brampton."

"Pleased to meet you," he said. "I understand you were kidnapped, and Levi and his men rescued you."

"As long as you include Ice in that category, then, yes."

Ice smiled to show him she wasn't really offended.

He tilted his head her way in acknowledgment, then resumed speaking to Lissa. "However, as you guessed, they all have been here many a time and have rooms assigned. I will take you to yours. If you will follow me, please."

She grinned. Stone leaned against the open entryway to the living room. As she walked past him, she said, "I get the shower before you."

"Better save some water," he said. "Tanks like me take a

lot to clean up."

"Better get there fast," she said. "I'm not even sure I re-member what hot water feels like."

She followed Charles upstairs, and instead of going left, he took a right. He opened the door to a bedroom that looked out over the backyard. It was a beautiful room with a very Victorian style and a four-poster bed. She stopped and gazed at the bed. "What's wrong with me? This is absolutely gorgeous."

"How very American. Why would anything have to be wrong with you in order to enjoy something our ancestors knew very well how to build and enjoy themselves?" Charles's tone was laughing, yet curious.

She turned and smiled at him. "So true. It's missing a princess dress, and a part of me just seems to think that would be perfect right now. And yet the other part of me says, I should be an adult and let all this go. It's like a dream for a child, and I'm supposed to be all grown-up."

He patted her on the shoulder and said, "No, my dear. It's for discerning people who enjoy the good things in life and who want the very best sleep they can get. Now the bathroom is through there." He motioned to the small door on the far side that she hadn't seen until now. "I understand you have no clothing so we will need to make arrangements for that. However, in the meantime, I'm hoping something in those drawers will fit at least temporarily. Feel free to look."

Walking toward the bedroom door, he added, "Towels are in the bathroom. Please make yourself at home." With a smile he stepped from the room and closed the door behind him.

She did a twirl, then added a little skip and a hop. She

was so damn happy to be here.

This room was fantastic. She couldn't imagine actually having something like this for herself all the time. But for right now, the little girl inside jumped for joy. Her dad would frown and call this frivolous and a waste of money.

She couldn't agree more. And she loved every penny spent on it.

With a huge grin, she headed to the bathroom and the hot water waiting for her. She could finally soak the dried blood off her hair and clean the wound on her forehead. Thankfully it was minor. She didn't know what the hot water system was like here, but she knew one thing. Stone was right. It would take a lot of water to clean his body. She wanted to get in her shower first.

Of course, if she wanted to be frugal and save money for her host, she could have invited Stone to share the shower with her.

That would be fun.

More fun would be the look on his face. Her grin widened. Just the thought of all that heavy muscle was enough to make her body warm. He was deadly.

Since when did she go for the strong silent type?

Since she'd met Stone.

"INTERESTING WOMAN," HARRISON said at Stone's side.

"That she is." Stone turned and faced the rest of the crew. "Are we waiting for anything or can we head to our rooms and grab showers? Of course a change of clothes would be nice."

"Our bags won't be here for a few hours," Levi said. "With any luck they will arrive by the time we wake up in the morning. Charles knows they are on the way." He stood up, reaching out a hand for Ice.

Stone studied the pallor on her face and realized they were all feeling the time change.

"We're heading to bed," Levi said easily. "We'll see you in the morning."

Stone watched as his two best friends headed up the stairs. He was happy for them. They were finally working things out. They'd always been a matched set. But happily for them, they'd become stronger than ever.

What a joy to be with them now. It hadn't been bad before, but it hurt seeing them at a crossroad. The team wanted to help them but was unable to do anything but stand by in silent support and hope they worked their issues out.

Stone wanted to take off his prosthesis and ease up his leg. With a wave at the rest of the guys, he climbed the stairs. They'd all be following him soon enough. He headed into the same room he had had the last time.

Charles was old military. He'd inherited this place from his parents. It hadn't taken long for all his old buddies to find out the space was available for those in need. No questions asked.

Even better, Charles collected great intel for them. He had a lot of connections in London. They often had to call on him for information. Some kind of arrangement had been reached between Levi and Charles; Stone didn't know exactly what it was, but there never seemed to be any hardship, so obviously the agreement worked for them both.

Stone and Levi had been tight in the military; the men in a unit are like none other. Stone considered himself lucky to have been under Levi's command and had never once blamed him for the mess they'd ended up in. Not his fault.

Betrayal happened. In pulling this company together, Levi had breathed new life into his unit. Even bringing Stone in—trusting that he'd get himself on his feet and still be a viable member of the team.

He'd do anything for Levi and the others. But it had been a damn hard fight to get back here. On the outside he seemed like Mr. Invincible. On the inside he knew he was a mess. He walked into his room relieved nobody else would be sharing it with him this time.

He could use the private space. He quickly stripped off his clothing and sat down on the bed. He removed his prosthesis and shuddered with relief. No matter how short or long a time he wore it, it was always a relief to take it off.

In his gear was a salve for the stump, but he'd do without it for the night. He needed a shower first. Standing up, he hopped lightly to the bathroom and stepped inside.

With the hot water pouring down his back, he let his stress ease, and slowly relaxed. Only afterward, standing in front of the mirror and shaving, he thought he heard a knock on his door.

"Hang on," he called. He quickly slipped on his prosthesis and walked to the door, a towel around his waist. He opened it to find Lissa, wearing a robe of some kind.

"Oh, hi." She looked apologetic. "I'm across the hallway. I thought it was your room but wasn't sure."

"You should be sound asleep." He stood quietly studying her.

She winced. "I know, and I hate to bother you, but is there any place to get food?" She leaned forward and said in a low voice, "I have to eat often or my blood sugar drops and I pass out."

"Oh, not good. How bad is it, right now?"

"Bad enough." She looked down toward the stairs. "I

was kind of hoping that maybe if you're familiar with this area, you knew a place to go and get something to eat. The other problem is, I honestly don't have any money." This time her tone of voice was apologetic, almost ashamed.

He reached out a hand and rubbed her shoulder. "It's all right. I'm sure we can get some food downstairs." He stepped back slightly. "Give me a minute to get changed."

"If you don't mind, I'd appreciate it," she said in a small voice, looking around. "I'd ask Charles, but I don't have a clue where to find him."

"Not to worry. Just give me a minute." He didn't want to close the door in her face, but he was hardly dressed to bring her inside the room.

She stood with her arms wrapped around her chest, but finally she nodded. "Go. I'll be fine."

"I'm not so sure about that," he said, "but I won't be long." He closed the door and walked to where his clothes lay on the ground. He didn't have a spare set, but he gave his a quick shake, slipped on his jeans, put on his T-shirt and socks, and headed to the doorway. He opened the door and stepped out.

The hallway was empty.

He frowned, hating the instant suspicion. Where was she? Why was she not here? And had something happened to her?

Which was her bedroom? He frowned as he studied the rooms, trying to remember which one was the most unused. She'd said she was across the hallway from him.

He walked there and knocked on the door. No answer.

Dammit, where was she?

Suddenly the door opened in front of him.

And there she was. A bright smile on her face.

Chapter 6

L ISSA SMILED UP at Stone. "Thank you," she said. "I felt stupid standing in the hallway alone so I went to my room to wait."

"No worries. I was just concerned something had happened to you." He motioned to the stairway. "Shall we?"

She walked down the stairs ahead of him. At the bottom she waited for him to join her. "Where to?"

He motioned to a doorway on the left. "We'll go through here. The kitchen is on the other side."

"Are you sure it's okay if we scavenge for food?" She looked around. "I feel like I'm sneaking around a stranger's house, and that makes me very uncomfortable. Wouldn't it be better to go out and grab a meal?"

He laughed. "It's fine. I'm sure Charles probably hears us even now. He's likely to be in the kitchen, waiting for us."

"Oh, dear. That would make me feel even worse," she exclaimed quietly. "I don't want to disturb the poor man. We already woke him up in the middle of the night to get in."

"Not to worry." Charles suddenly stood in front of them. Dressed in a smoking jacket and pajama pants with big slippers, he looked distinguished and ... adorable.

"I'm sorry if we woke you," she whispered. Not what she wanted to do at all. This had gone from embarrassing to selfish. "We should have just stepped out and found a place to eat."

"That wouldn't have worked. The security is tight in this place." Charles offered a small smile. "I change it regularly so you'd have set off the alarms and woken me anyway." He motioned in front of him. "There are, however, meat pies and multiple other dishes in there."

As they entered the kitchen, he said, "You weren't the only ones hungry." He walked to the fridge. "Some of the men needed to eat before they went to bed as well. In fact, I apologize. I should have offered you something as soon as you arrived. I am sorry for the oversight."

She sat down and watched as he pulled out food from some of the cupboards and fridge. And there was a lot of it. "Do you think we should ask anyone else?" she murmured to Stone. "I would feel bad if others went to bed hungry."

His smile was slow to come but when it did finally shine, it was a thing of beauty.

She forgot to chew she was so enraptured. When she finally remembered, she swallowed hard and said, "You should come with a warning."

He stopped chewing and stared at her.

She laughed. "I guess that surprised you." She nodded her thanks as Charles brought a glass of milk to her. She smiled at the childhood treat. "Are you sure you won't join us, Charles?"

"No, my dear, I ate hours ago."

Of course he did. He ate at a normal mealtime before his company ruined his evening. She forked another bite of meat pie. "This is delicious."

"I'm glad you're enjoying it. It was freshly made today. A touch strong on the nutmeg, do you think?"

"It's wonderful," she murmured around a mouthful of meat and spices wrapped in pastry. "Lovely."

He smiled quietly and cut her a second piece, placing it on her plate without asking.

So focused on her food, she didn't realize when Charles left.

Finally she laid down her fork and leaned back, contented. "That was so good."

Stone was still eating his third piece of meat pie. She watched the big man as he took bite after bite. He was careful and methodical but also showed appreciation for every piece.

He was a fascinating male. She picked up her glass of milk and took a sip, then quickly collected the dishes she'd used and carried them to the sink. She suspected a dishwasher was here, but she'd rather do them by hand. She cleaned up her dishes, then returned for the few Stone had used.

"Are you done?" she asked, studying the empty plate in front of him.

"Stuffed." He lifted his plate and used the table to stand.

Interesting. He'd made several other moves that she'd seen but hadn't really noticed as being different. The little incidences were adding up—in a good way. Then she remembered seeing him limp every so often.

She sat down suddenly. "Are you hurt?"

He frowned. Then shook his head. "I'm fine. Why do you ask?"

When she gazed at his bloody shirt, he smiled and said, "Not to worry. Like you, I don't have clean clothes to change into."

"Right. But something is wrong. I noticed it earlier, but wasn't sure what I was seeing."

"I'm not sure what you're seeing now," he said with a frown furrowing his forehead. "I'm fine."

She bit her lower lip and nodded. If he didn't want to talk, she wasn't going to push it. He was entitled to his secrets. She had a few she didn't want to drag from the closet either.

He stood straight and said, "Are you ready to sleep now?"

"I think so."

He held out his hand.

She placed hers in it and let him lead her to the stairs. "I'm not sure I would have found the kitchen on my own."

"Sure you would have. You traveled halfway around the world to help others. This wouldn't have been a problem."

"Maybe, but that seems a full world away now. Something about being kidnapped has me feeling less confident and secure in my own abilities." She stopped at the top of the stairs and said, "I don't like it."

SOMETHING ABOUT THE tone of her voice made him look at her twice. "Will you be okay tonight?"

She reached out for her bedroom doorknob and said, "I'd be pretty damn sad if I'm in a house with so many men and not consider myself safe. I'm inside, safe, secure, and surrounded by bodyguards."

She tossed him an overly bright smile and walked into her room. "Have a good night. See you in the morning."

She closed the door gently in his face. Frowning, he walked to his bedroom and opened the door. As he went to close it, he found himself studying hers.

Something about this bugged the hell out of him, but he

couldn't figure out what or why. Against his instincts, he went in his room, closed the door behind him, and walked to his bed. Still fully dressed, he lay down on top of the covers, crossing his hands underneath his head, and stared up at the ceiling. She hadn't acted any odder than she had already, and she wasn't all that odd. She was just unique.

He liked unique. But something else was there besides that. So what if she was afraid tonight? She should be fine. Like she said, the house was full of bodyguards. And there was no reason to think anybody was after her anyway.

Eventually he drifted off but found himself unable to get into a deep sleep. He rolled over in time to see his doorknob turn. Instantly he was awake and up. Standing behind the door, hidden from whoever was coming in, he waited.

The door opened just enough that it unlatched. But it moved back and forth ever-so-slightly, as if somebody stood on the other side, deciding if they should open it or not. Then he knew.

In a quiet voice he said, "Lissa?"

Instantly the door opened wide, and she poked her head around. "Are you awake?"

The relief in her voice tugged at his heart. He stepped from behind the door, startling her. She took several steps back into the hallway, but he tugged her forward into his room quickly and closed the door behind her. The last thing he wanted was the rest of the house to be awake and aware. "What's wrong?"

Eyes downcast, she shrugged. He stepped to the side, and the moonlight from the window caught her face, and he could see the shine of her skin. He reached up a hand and stroked the damp tendrils of hair. "You had a nightmare, didn't you?"

She raised her gaze to him, her lower lip trembling, and nodded. "It just seems so unreal," she began. "I couldn't believe all this happened. I had to make sure I wasn't dreaming and that you were actually here. That *somebody* was here."

And he realized they'd made a tactical mistake. They should've had her share a room with Ice.

She wouldn't have been alone then. On the other hand maybe this way he'd benefit too.

He wasn't averse to sharing his bed for the night. Especially if it meant they could both get some decent sleep. He knew that was why he had yet to rest. And he needed to because who knew what tomorrow would bring. He wrapped a gentle arm around her shoulder and tugged her toward the bed.

"You can stay in my bed tonight."

She stopped and looked at him hopefully. "You sure? You don't mind?"

Half in exasperation and half in humor he said, "No, I don't mind. Yes, I'm sure. I offered. And, yes, we're just going to sleep, even though you didn't ask."

He gave her a push toward the bed, and, with a big grin, she rushed to the side he had not been sleeping on, crawling quickly under the covers.

She looked at his still-made side of the bed and asked, "Weren't you sleeping?"

He walked closer and sat down. For the first time he was feeling a little unsure. He shrugged and said, "Trying to."

She patted his shoulder. "That's okay. I'll keep you safe."

He gave a bark of laughter and lay down on top of the covers beside her. "I'd like to see that."

She curled up in a ball beside him and murmured, "You

can get under the covers, you know. You would sleep better if you took off your T-shirt."

He crossed his arms over his belly and said, "I'm fine. Go to sleep."

"You're better than fine, but you'd sleep a whole lot better if you took off the prosthetic limb too." She gave a great big yawn before rolling to face the other side of the room. "I'm beat."

He lay still as her words whispered into his head. Of course she recognized he was missing a leg. Why did that surprise him? Not many people mentioned it, that's why. In fact, no one outside the team and Jackson ever did. But then again, he hung around everybody who knew the details. Not like it was a secret back at the compound. Still, he was relieved that she knew and was okay with it.

As he lay here, he realized he was a fool. The damn thing was chafing his stump, and he really would like to get it off. He waited another few minutes to make sure she was sleeping, then he sat up, pulled off his T-shirt, slipped off his jeans—leaving himself in boxers—and unclipped the prosthesis, dropping it all to the floor. With a quick flick, he had the blankets over him, then he stretched out under the covers.

Much better. With a smile on his face he fell into an easy sleep.

Chapter 7

S HE WOKE ALONE but with a sense of security she hadn't had in a hell of a long time. She turned on her back in the big bed, her hand falling on the warm spot where Stone had lain. She wondered if he'd ever gotten comfortable enough to take off the prosthesis.

She got up, made her side of the bed, and crept to the doorway. Given that she'd spent the night in his room, she didn't want him to be teased by the others or to have anyone get the wrong idea, so she wanted to return to her room without anybody seeing her.

Listening from inside his room, she couldn't hear anyone yet. She opened the door, saw the hallway was empty, and quickly made her way to her room. She went straight to the drawers where Charles had said there would be clothing for her. She could definitely use something clean to wear.

She found jeans, some kind of a yoga-looking pants, T-shirts with long sleeves ... In fact, a whole collection of clothing was here. But nothing in the way of underclothes. Still, probably for the best. She wasn't sure how she felt about wearing somebody else's underwear. She picked a pair of pants and went with a T-shirt that should fit and dressed quickly. Given that she was in London, and, from the window, it was rainy, she found a cardigan that she quickly put on over her T-shirt. She was still adapting to the temperatures.

Although she'd finally slept, she knew she would need a lot more rest. She didn't know what today would bring, and she wanted to be prepared.

She made her way downstairs into the kitchen. The group of men were already seated, enjoying breakfast, including Stone. He patted the seat beside him, and, with a smile, she sat down.

"I'm not sure we should meet again here. Seems like just a few hours." Several people stopped and looked up at her. She winced. "Maybe I wasn't supposed to say anything, but Charles was kind enough to feed me last night."

"Good for Charles," Levi said. "I know most of the men had something to eat before sleeping." He waved at the tableful of food. "Help yourself. Charles is manning the stove. I believe bacon and eggs are coming, if you want some."

And, boy, did she. It might only have been a few hours, but she was starving again. How the hell did that happen?

By the time breakfast was over, she felt comfortable with the group once more. "What's on tap for today?"

"Waiting on the luggage. And then flying home."

"Yay," she said with a smile.

Levi's phone rang, which he answered right away. "What?" His gaze immediately zipped toward Lissa. "Right. We'll bring her in the next couple hours. What about the other luggage?"

She looked around the table quickly and realized Kevin and Susan weren't here. She turned to look at Stone and asked in a very low voice, "Are Susan and Kevin okay?"

He shook his head. "Susan was taken to the hospital this morning. Kevin's with her."

She was stunned at what she'd already missed. She reached for his wrist, twisted it so she could see the time. It was nine o'clock. "Good Lord, when was that?"

"They were gone by six-thirty this morning," he said calmly. "Nothing you could do. She's getting the best care possible. And, yes, you can see them later if the hospital allows."

Levi got off the phone just then and turned to Lissa. "What was in your luggage?"

At the hard tone in his voice, her mouth dropped open. "Just the basics. A couple pairs of pants and shirts, and a hoodie." She raised her hands in an "I don't know" motion, adding, "Toiletries, shampoo, a little bit of makeup, deodorant, and a book. I had an iPod but my cell phone is here with me." She fished it from her pocket and put it on the table. "I don't even know why I keep it. It doesn't work."

Stone immediately picked it up and popped out the battery, checking it. He put it back together and played with its buttons.

"It turns on but won't send or receive, and I can't call out. I should grab my contacts off there before I can't get them any longer. I just need a pen and paper." She watched him for a moment, then shrugged, turning her gaze to Levi. "What's wrong?"

"We have to return to customs. Something suspicious has been found in your luggage. They also want to see anything that you had on you when you came through."

She raised her eyes and froze. "Well, my dirty clothes are still upstairs."

Ice spoke up quietly. "I'm sure it's nothing. We'll head down, clear things up, and carry on. We all need our luggage, but yours came in separately from the refugee camp.

Or did you have a bag at the rebel compound where you were held?"

She shrugged. "Two bags were snatched up with us. One of Susan's and also a bag with first aid kits. But I lost track of both almost immediately. It was all very confusing. I never saw the same person twice, no matter the luggage."

"I have to ask before this gets any further," Levi said in a hard voice. "And you need to tell me right now if you were carrying anything that you shouldn't have been."

She stared at him in surprise and asked cautiously, "Like what?"

"Well, drugs for one."

She sat back, stunned. "I don't do drugs."

"Anything else? Money, weapons?"

"No!" she said in shock. "Nothing like that. I was there to give humanitarian aid, not to run drugs." She shook her head. "It's not like drugs were there anyway. It's not something anyone could get locally. I never saw anything in the clinics where I was working."

Ice asked, "I know this stuff isn't easy to consider, but what about Kevin and Susan?"

Instantly Lissa shook her head. "Oh, no. I never saw them doing anything like that."

Levi straightened from the table and said, "We'll have to deal with this. Not all of us though. Lissa, you and Stone are coming with us, and we'll bring Harrison too. Ice will stay here and await the arrival of the other luggage as well as keep the lines of communication open."

To Lissa that all sounded normal. But the hard glance Levi shot Ice and the blank look on her face said something else entirely.

WHAT THE HELL? Something was going on. Yet, if he could get the others alone, he might be able to find out. But as long as she was beside him, they weren't saying anything. He couldn't blame them if their suspicions fell on her shoulders right now. They had put their necks out to rescue her, but if she was doing something illegal, that could get them all in a shitload of trouble.

He couldn't see it. But he'd been wrong before.

They walked out to the vehicle waiting for them. It wasn't a cab, but the driver obviously was expecting them. In the backseat Stone watched as Lissa nervously clenched her fingers together.

In a low voice she said to him, "I swear I didn't do anything wrong."

He studied the look on her face and what he knew of the tone in her voice. Words might lie, but body language really didn't. It took a consummate professional to pull that off. And he believed her. He reached over and patted her knee gently. "We'll get to the bottom of this. Don't you worry."

She gave a strangled laugh. "How am I not supposed to? They found something in my backpack. Like, what the hell, Stone? Anybody could have put something in my bag. It wasn't even in my possession for the last however long."

"And that's exactly what we'll tell them," Levi said. At least he was no longer the cold stranger she'd seen earlier. Now he looked ready to listen to her.

"Will they believe me?" she asked in a small voice.

"We can vouch for the time you were with us," Levi said with certainty. "And like you said, your bag was not with you for many days. So that will add up to someone else being involved."

"Any chance my passport will be there?"

"No, but we've taken care of that. As soon as we knew where you were, arrangements were made to get you home safely. It would be easier if you had it now, but it's not the end of the world that you don't."

Stone settled back. The traffic was rough outside. He was glad he wasn't driving. If he was forced to navigate these congested streets, he'd like to drive a Hummer. At least then everyone would get the hell out of his way. Instead, the cars were cutting off their driver on a consistent basis.

As he stared out the window, wondering what the hell customs had found in her bags, a small hand worked its way under his palm. He looked at her. She stared out the window, chewing on her bottom lip. Instantly he wrapped her hand in his and gently stroked his thumb across the top, noting how smooth her skin was, how very feminine. His was more of a meat fest. He could crush the bones in her fingers without even thinking about it. "It'll be okay."

When he squeezed her fingers, she squeezed back, never saying a word. She seemed to relax a little bit though.

Once there, they made their way to the customs office. They were met by somebody Levi knew. And then Stone realized Charles was here too. Stone hadn't seen Charles leave the house. Stone frowned and asked Levi, "How the hell did Charles get here?"

"He left ahead of us, heading to the hospital. I called him as soon as we knew there was a problem. He used to work for MI6."

"Well, that's good. Maybe."

They stood and waited until they were led into another room. The four of them sat down in a chair and waited some more. Only Lissa fidgeted, and Stone couldn't blame her.

Finally the door opened, and a man walked in with a file

folder. He sat down at the table opposite them, opened the file, and spread out pictures. It appeared to be photos of clothing, personal effects, and a bag. Lissa leaned forward and said, "That's my bag."

And that started the volley of questions. When had she last seen her bag? Where had she? Did she know who had had contact with it? The questions just went on and on and on.

Finally she threw up her hands and said, "I don't know what else I can tell you. I saw the two bags right after being kidnapped. I thought one was Susan's, but I can't be sure. I never saw it again. As for mine, they were in my quarters in the refugee camp, as far as I know. Again, I was kidnapped and have no idea what happened to anything with us or what was left behind." She shrugged and said, "Honestly I thought I'd never see any of my belongings again. Everything was replaceable."

After that followed a series of questions about her father, family life, business interests, political leanings, and even her religion. With every question she got quieter and quieter.

Stone sympathized, but there was no point in showing that right now. They'd been responsible for entering a foreign country and plucking her from it. This needed to be cleared up right now.

A knock sounded on the door, and without waiting for the okay to enter, the door opened to admit Charles. He came in and handed Levi a stack of documents. "These are her passport and visas—all her documentation." He glanced at Lissa, appearing to note the pallor in her face. "Lissa, I'm afraid that anything in your bag is now forfeit."

"I don't care," she said tiredly. "I don't know what you guys found in my stuff, but I can guarantee you I didn't put any contraband in there."

Abruptly the man on the other side of the table who had been asking so many questions stood and said, "You're all free to go."

Stone wanted to laugh at the sudden sag in her shoulders as she understood that she was no longer being held. He stood and motioned for her to get up. They stepped from the room.

Charles, now with them, said, "I suggest we take her somewhere so she can grab some clothing and see if we can get you all on the same flight this afternoon."

"I don't really care about new clothing. Please, can I just go home?"

Stone reached up and rubbed her shoulder. "Soon. Very soon."

But he doubted it would be soon enough to suit her.

Chapter 8

FOR SOME REASON she hadn't expected they would be
flying commercial, although she wasn't sure what other
options there were. The large group was spread out up and
down the rows of seats. She'd been afraid she would get
stuck beside one of the other men, but she felt luck was on
her side that she was sitting beside Stone. As she glanced at
his bland face, she thought maybe that had nothing to do
with it.

As the plane taxied down the runway, she leaned over
and said, "Thank you."

"You're welcome."

From the twinkle she saw in his eye, she knew he understood what she was thanking him for.

He really was a nice man. She also knew she wouldn't be
completely relaxed until they cleared customs in the States,
and she was free and clear.

They'd opted not to go shopping in London, so she was
still wearing the clothes Charles generously donated to the
cause. She made a mental note to send him something nice
as a thank you when she got home.

Not exactly how she thought her first trip to London
would go. But after that customs visit, she was a whole lot
less inclined to return.

She leaned back in her seat and closed her eyes. It would

be a long flight home.

Although it was, it wasn't as bad as she thought. She copied her contact list off her phone onto a napkin. Then it didn't matter if she couldn't use this phone; she could still contact her friends when she got a replacement. With the flight attendants coming up and down the aisle with coffee, drinks, and snacks, along with Stone beside her the whole way, the trip was actually fairly fast. They landed in New York, and just like that, they cleared customs.

When she finally stood on the other side of customs, she beamed with joy. "Wow, that went a lot better than I thought it would."

"Not everything is full of those bumps in life," Ice said. "Sometimes things actually go smoothly."

It hadn't occurred to Lissa to ask what they were doing after getting her here. She turned to study Stone and felt her heart jerk. "Am I saying good-bye to you guys here?"

"Three of the unit will be heading back to base," Levi said. "Four of us are taking you home."

"And whose home would that be? My home or my parents'?"

Everyone stopped. Levi said in a conversational tone that ended with a question, "Your father said you lived at his home. In Colorado."

"Of course he did. Whereas I actually have a townhouse in the suburbs of Houston, Texas."

Silence.

"In that case," Levi said slowly, "I'm hoping we can get your cooperation to visit your parents so we can complete this, and then we'll see about getting you to Texas."

"Are the tickets already booked for Colorado?"

"Yes. Like I said, for the four of us. The rest of the crew is going home."

"And where's home for the rest of you?" she asked curiously. And as hard as she tried not to, her gaze drifted toward Stone.

His lips quirked. "Texas."

She beamed. "Perfect. So can I go home with you guys, please?" she asked in a pleading tone. "I don't want to stay at my parents' place any longer than I have to. I can pay you back the ticket price."

At that, Levi nodded. "We can change yours so you travel with us all the way there." He smiled. "Your father is paying for these flights though."

"Then don't tell him one of those is for me. He'll cancel it before we ever get out of the house if he knows."

They landed in Denver and were still in the airport several hours later.

She wondered if she'd ever get to her home. Each leg of this journey was taking more out of her. It felt like soon there'd be nothing left of her.

Standing in the airport lobby, she recognized the limousine as it pulled up in front of the wall of doors.

"Typical, Father." She got in the back with the others.

The trip was less than twenty minutes, but it helped that there was mostly no traffic. As they pulled up to the family home, she studied the austereness of the residence. An imposing big brick structure with nothing to soften the heavy lines. "He really should move to London. That would suit him."

The driver, a man she didn't know, came around to open the door for her. She waited until they'd all exited the limo before walking up to the front door.

It opened before they made it to the porch.

Her father stood in the doorway, his arms crossed as he glared at her. She stepped forward in front of the team and said, "Hello, Father."

"There you are. Are you done causing trouble?"

She heard the hisses of surprise behind her. But it would take a lot for her father's words to hurt her anymore. "As I didn't ask to be kidnapped, nor did I do anything to cause this, I hardly think it's fair that you blame me for it." She motioned at the open doors behind him. "Are we going in, or am I saying good-bye right here?"

His eyebrows soared, and the anger in his face dropped away. "What do you mean? You're leaving? You can't leave now," he protested. Still he glared at the others, then stepped back from the doorway. "Come in. Come in."

Levi entered first, and the others followed.

Lissa stood outside on the big porch and wondered if there was any way to disappear. But with her father glaring at her, and Stone standing there waiting, she didn't think so.

Oh, well, might as well face the music right now rather than later.

They walked into the living room. As Lissa stepped around in front of the others, she caught sight of her mother sitting beside the fireplace, poised perfectly, as if for photographs. But so not as a mother greeting a daughter who had just returned from a harrowing kidnapping experience.

Lissa stepped into the middle of the room and said, "Hello, Mother. You're looking well."

Her mother stood and smiled prettily. "Thank you. You're looking better than I expected, but oh, dear, stitches. You know that will leave a scar," she said reprovingly.

"I'm fine, thank you. No need to worry now that I'm home safe."

There, the polite conversation was done. Maybe she could leave now. As she glanced around, she caught sight of Stone's frown. She slightly rolled her eyes as if to say, *I told you so.*

"She was very brave and handled herself well under the circumstances," Stone said in a low voice.

Her mother gave a delicate shudder. "She goes on these excursions, putting herself in danger, and it's very trying for us all."

This time Lissa did roll her eyes. Of course it was trying for everyone but more so for Lissa, not her mother. All it did was interrupt her mother's schedule and force her to adjust.

Her father who had left, reappeared suddenly. He handed an envelope to Levi. "A bonus. And you have my deepest thanks for rescuing my daughter."

The two men shook hands. In her father's typical style, he completely passed over Ice who stood at Levi's side as he proceeded to shake Harrison and Stone's hands.

Her eyes twinkling, she prodded her father. "Don't forget about Ice, Dad. She's one of the main members of their unit."

Her father looked startled at the comment or maybe at the unusual name but moved in front of her, appearing to be amiable about shaking her hand too.

Ice glanced at Lissa, a glint of humor in her eye as she said, "Lovely to have met you, Lissa. You've been very brave throughout this whole event."

"That's a good one. I survived. That's about all I can say. Except that I wouldn't have without you guys. I'll miss you," she admitted warmly.

She heard her mother's disdainful sniffle behind her. Lissa stiffened at the rebuke, and her gaze caught Stone's once again.

This group was more her kind of people. She was a misfit in her family and always had been. She turned to her father and said, "Now what, Father?" He'd always orchestrated her life. She had no doubt he'd planned her return down to the smallest detail.

"I'm sure you're tired. Go to your room and rest," he said in a tone that brooked no argument. "We'll talk in the morning."

She knew how that worked. Instantly she ran up the stairs. The obedient returning daughter. *Like hell.*

Thankfully, she knew this house well. She heard her father at the front door saying good-bye to the team and realized she had no time.

She just hoped they could stall long enough so she could sneak out the rear and come around to the front without being seen. They knew she had a ticket booked to go home to Texas with them. She did not want to miss that flight. Nor did she want to stay here.

At the top of stairs was the fire escape out the back. She was on that, skittering down as fast as she could. Hitting the ground running, she came around to the side of the property. The limo was already driving around the circular drive that would take the big vehicle to the main road.

She cut a corner across the front yard and dashed into the center of the road.

She didn't dare look at the front door to see if her father was still standing there. She was counting on the fact that he would not watch the vehicle leave.

The black limousine hit the brakes. Thankfully, he hadn't been going very fast so the squeal wasn't enough to raise alarms inside the house. The driver frowned as he looked through the windshield.

The rear passenger door opened, and Stone stepped out, a hard look on his face. "Are you nuts? That's a great way to get yourself killed."

She dashed to his side, reaching up to kiss him on the cheek. "I missed you too."

She dove inside the vehicle and sat on the front seat facing them, then pounded the glass lightly to tell the driver to move. With an impudent grin, she glanced at the others. "So, what did you think of my father?"

STONE KEPT HIS thoughts to himself. A lot of comments rolled around in his head, but his mother had taught him a few simple commands to follow in life. One of them was if he couldn't say anything nice, don't say anything at all.

And there was nothing nice about his thoughts right now.

In fact, if he had Lissa's father in front of him, Stone would be hard pressed to hold his fists back. And as for that doll of a mother …

Well, he had no words.

Apparently nobody else in the vehicle could voice their feelings either because complete silence reigned.

Lissa laughed. "That's all right. It's exactly how I feel too."

She settled down into the vehicle and tucked her knees up against her chest. She stared out the window, watching as the miles passed. Stone studied her features, but they were blank, as if she herself didn't know what to think. He sensed a finality in her and wondered if she'd ever return to her parents' house.

"What will your father do to you for sneaking out?" Ice asked.

Lissa turned to her. "Who said I had to sneak?" She turned her gaze back out the window for a long time. Then she said, "I have no idea. He should be used to me fighting his dictates, but he always seems surprised when he gives orders and I refuse."

"Why not stay a little while with your parents?" Harrison asked. "I don't mean any offense. I just have trouble with you not wanting to at least reassure them that you're okay after what you've been through."

"And I did that," she said quietly. "As you can see, it's

not like they wanted to spend any time with me. I was ordered to my room to stay for the night. Father would speak with me in the morning, when he had time. But what I can tell you from past experience is, he would order me to his office the next day, and he would give me a complete dressing down for my actions. After that I'd be ordered back to my room. I did not need to listen to that again."

Harrison nodded. "As long as you know for sure that's what would happen."

"What about your mother? Has she ever intervened?" Ice asked. "I don't have a mother or haven't for a long time, but my father and I are close. I can't imagine not having the kind of relationship that we have."

"I can't imagine having what you must have," Lissa said. "Honestly, I don't know anything other than our cold existence. I was never hugged or held, except by my nannies. I wasn't allowed to eat at the same dinner table until I was *old enough*. I went to boarding school because it was more convenient for them, so they didn't have to drive me anywhere or deal with me on weekends."

She glanced from one face to the other and finally landed on Stone. "It wasn't so bad," she said quietly. "I made friends in school. Every once in a while I would go to their place for holidays." She turned to stare out the window again. "In fact, it was nicer at boarding school than it was at home."

Stone stared down at his open hands resting on his lap. They were open to prevent him from clenching them into fists and pounding something. The only thing available to pound was the vehicle, and he didn't want to end up dealing with her father over that.

Chapter 9

B Y THE TIME they got on to the next flight, she was too tired to talk. Stone once again sat beside her, and she made absolutely no apologies for curling up and resting her head against his broad shoulder and closing her eyes.

The only thing that bothered her was her heart taking on the fear of the approaching good-bye.

She was not looking forward to that.

Somehow she had become accustomed to being with Stone, but she didn't get close to people easily. And yet somehow she felt attached to him. He'd also been there with her for the last couple days, and she would find it very hard to let him go. Yet he had a life. *Remember,* she told herself, *she was just a job.* Although they might both live in Texas, that didn't mean he was interested.

"Wake up, Lissa."

She straightened and stared at him blurry-eyed. "Are we landing now?"

He nodded. "Will be. We started our descent. We'll be down in ten minutes."

She nodded and reached up to cover her mouth with her hand as she yawned. "Oh, man, am I tired."

"It's been a long trip home," he said. "You'll need a couple days to relax."

"I still have to get home," she said. "That means trying

to find a taxi at this hour. And I don't think I have keys to my house anymore."

"Didn't you hide a set?" he asked with one eyebrow raised.

"No. I left the spares with Marge so she could get in and check my mail." She made a face. "Now to find a way to break in. Part of me wants to say I hope I left a window open, but another knows damn well I better not have." She slumped into her seat, depressed as all hell now. "Goddammit."

"Don't worry about it. We'll figure it out."

"You mean, I'll have to. You'll head off to your home, back to your job. Me? I need to go home and find a way to start my life all over again." She hated the note of bitterness in her tone, but right now, a little bit too much had happened over an incredibly long series of days. All she wanted was to go home and crash on her bed. The fact that she probably couldn't even get into her own house ... Talk about a grand finale. And yet, because of him, she had a life. She needed to stop whining and appreciate what she had.

"I'm not leaving you after all that we've done so far. I need to be sure you'll be okay," he said in exasperation. "You are just over an hour's drive from my home. I'll take you to your place first. We'll see if we can get you inside. If not, we'll look at other options."

Feeling shaky but relieved, she threw her arms around him and gave him a big hug. "Thank you so much. I have to admit I was feeling really nervous about this last bit. And I shouldn't be," she exclaimed. "I finally get to go home."

He reached out and grabbed her hand. "Hold that thought. We'll get you there probably in about an hour and a half, depending on how much trouble we have getting off the airplane. But considering the minimal baggage you have, there should be absolutely no problem."

She stood outside the airport exit not knowing what to do. For the first damn time in a long while she was home. The team was in sight, and she didn't want to be separated. Nerves? Or just plain fear? She didn't know.

She turned to glance behind her. Stone was talking with the others. Finally some kind of an agreement was made. Some shoulder slapping, smiles, and then the other three turned in another direction.

Stone came toward her. "Okay, we have two vehicles here. They will take one and go home, and I will take you to your place and then go home myself."

She watched the other three retreat, feeling a sadness she hadn't expected. "You sure it's okay with them? Shouldn't you be going home with them?"

"Actually they were all coming with me," he said. "But as this should be a simple trip to get you into your house, they decided to go home themselves." He wrapped an arm around her shoulders as they walked to the parking lot. "I'll keep them updated. If there's any difficulty, they'll be here."

It took a moment, which she put down to tiredness, before the statement actually penetrated her foggy brain. "What do you mean by 'difficulty'?"

"I don't mean anything."

Before too long, he had her safely ensconced inside the passenger seat of a Jeep. She laughed when she got in. "I always wanted to ride in one of these but never have."

"You have a car?"

"Yes." She winced. "I have a Toyota Prius."

"Interesting choice."

"Well, I do care about the environment, and my daddy

was extremely against it." She laughed. "As I look back at my life, it seems like everything I've done has been to spite him." She gave her head a shake. "Definitely time to grow up."

"There's time for that," he said comfortably. "If you had stayed at your parents' house last night, what would you be facing now? And how much trouble would you have getting home to your own place now?"

"I don't have any money on me so I couldn't have gotten here without your help. God knows Father wouldn't have helped me. But, once I'm here, there's a telephone. Father can call me, but he does have friends in town who often come by to make sure I'm okay." She shrugged. "It's like he can't quite let go of that bit of control."

"He's a father," Stone said.

"That he is, but I doubt that has anything to do with it," she said quietly. She didn't mean to be mysterious, but there was just no understanding her father.

"Have they always been well-off?"

She nodded. "Old money, blue blood, and married wealthy. They did all the expected things. They even had a child. Unfortunately I seem to be the one part of their life that didn't turn out the way they expected."

Up ahead was the exit from the airport. "I need a few directions," he said.

"Oh, sorry. I am really tired. Take a left here. We're taking the Aberdeen exit about five minutes down the road."

"I know the area."

"Do you?"

He nodded. "I've spent a lot of years in Texas for one reason or another."

She studied his craggy features and said, "You know so much about me, and I don't know anything about you."

"Not a whole lot to know."

"The military is an interesting choice."

"Mom died of cancer six months before I enlisted. At that point I was lost. I was looking for a family. I signed up for BUD/S training and surprised myself by actually succeeding." He laughed. "At the time I felt I had found my perfect place.

"What is Buds?"

"Basic Underwater Demolition/SEAL training."

"But?"

"But what?"

"You said you thought you had found your perfect place *until* ..."

He turned to look at her. "Until we were on a mission and somebody betrayed us. We all took some pretty heavy physical damage. My unit, all four of us, had to leave the military because of it. I am the only one who lost a limb. Levi and I were hurt the worst. Rhodes and Merk had an easier time of it but not by much. Still we all survived and that's what counts."

He patted the dashboard. "But Levi was never anybody to stay down long. He'd always had it in the back of his head that, when his time was up in the military, he'd set up a private company and continue doing what we always did so well. So here we are."

"You don't have any family?"

"Only the family I work with."

Somehow that seemed really sad to her. Then again, how many times in her life had she wished to be an orphan? Maybe he had the better deal after all.

They turned off the highway, and she directed him through the small town toward her place. She was getting her second wind.

When they pulled into the driveway of her building, she smiled. The pretty Victorian look had always appealed to her. This place had seemed perfect for her at the time. And, in a way, maybe it still was. Except that, for some reason, she never spent any time here. She could change that now. Her traveling bug had certainly disappeared.

"Is this the place?" Stone turned to look at her.

"It certainly is." She hopped out and ran up to the front door. Sure enough it was locked. Although why she thought it wouldn't be, she had no idea. She ran down the stairs to Stone and said, "Let's check the back door."

He followed at a much slower pace. As she went around the building, she kept up a running stream of commentary about the place. "I bought it a couple years ago. At the time I really liked the pretty look to the place. It's just I haven't stayed here longer than a few months." She shrugged. "I've been traveling so much that it has not really ever seemed like home." She turned to look at him and froze.

His features had gone hard, a glint of steel to his gaze.

She reached out for his arm and stepped really close. "What the hell's the matter?"

He lifted an arm and pointed to the back door and the kitchen windows. "You tell me."

She turned to look at her kitchen and realized the windows were smashed in on both sides. The door, although closed, looked like it could flap in the wind. "Oh, my God! My place has been broken into."

"Did you have some kind of arrangement with the management to rent it out while you were gone?"

She shook her head. "No, I never wanted strangers in my house." She didn't make a move to get closer to the building.

Instead she just stood, clutching his arm. "This makes no sense."

"Why is that?" he said drily. "Tough times, small town, and an empty house for months on end ... I'm surprised it wasn't broken into before."

She turned to face him. "My friend Marge should have stopped by last night and checked it. She's been coming by once a week to collect my mail and to make sure the place was okay. She comes every Sunday night like clockwork."

"Can you check to see when she was here last?"

"I could, but she's sleeping right now, and I don't have a phone anymore," she said. "Why?"

"Just to make sure we have the correct time frame. It seems suspicious that you left this place empty for what, six months? Considering your friend was here recently, we have to assume she'd have noticed this damage, so it must have happened after her last trip here. We'll need to contact her next to confirm she came last night but if so ..."

"Eight months," she corrected.

"Right, for eight months. So we have to consider the possibility that now, on the day that you actually arrive here, your place is broken into."

Slowly her gaze went from the house to him, then back again. "Oh, my God! You think it's related, don't you?"

"LET'S JUST SAY it's not a coincidence I'm comfortable with," he said. "We had trouble with the London airport. Now you come home, and your place has been broken into. Not last week, but just now within roughly twenty-four hours of your return. Until we can confirm, we can consider this a working theory."

"Someone wants to scare me off?" She waved to her house. "It's not like I have much in valuables. I have a few pieces of secondhand furniture and some personal stuff. That's about it."

"*Hmm,*" was all he said, but his mind was churning. "Let's go take a look inside and see how bad the damage is."

He led the way, his boots crunching on the glass scattered on the steps. He reached into his pocket and pulled out a glove. Gently he opened the kitchen door. The screen came toward him easily enough, and she realized the exterior kitchen door had actually been broken in two.

He stepped inside and motioned for her to follow. "Don't touch anything," he warned.

"I won't," she muttered.

Beside him were the remains of a kitchen table and four chairs, all smashed to smithereens. He could hear her gasp in shock as they walked through the place. The contents of the cupboards looked to have been tossed; the fridge door was ajar, but even that looked to have been checked out. He walked toward the living room and stood stock-still.

Coming up behind him, she let out a gasp of outrage. "Oh, my God," she cried. "There was no need to destroy everything."

"This wasn't a normal burglary," he said. "Looks like they were searching for something."

"Or they were vandals," she snapped, "who just wanted to ruin things because they could."

He didn't say anything to that, but, as far as he was concerned, this looked like a whole lot more than a bunch of teenage hoods trying to make an impression.

He led the way upstairs and walked into her bedroom, finding exactly the same thing.

She pushed past him into the center of the room and stopped. Tears sprang to her eyes, and she put a hand to her temple. "Why?" she cried. "Why would anyone do this?"

Stone had more than a few ideas, but he didn't think she was ready to hear them. "I know it's a disaster, but can you possibly see if there's anything missing?"

She glanced at him to see if he was serious.

He nodded. "Yes, I'm serious."

She opened her arms wide. "I haven't been here for eight months. How am I supposed to remember what might've been here?"

"Were there any special mementos? Any money, jewelry, anything valuable at all?"

She shook her head. "Everything I have that is along that line is in a safety deposit box at the bank," she said. "I meant it when I said I was never here." She turned to study her bed. Not only had the bedding been slashed, the mattresses had been upended and apparently the tops cut open. "There was nothing here to find."

He waited while she walked through the room, talking out loud.

"This doesn't make any sense. This is more than the work of vandals. What could they possibly have been looking for?" She turned to him. "And why now?"

He kept silent, waiting. She'd get there eventually.

"No one knew I was coming home," she said, waving her arms. "So this couldn't be timed."

"Your dad said you were living at home with them." Stone shrugged. "But, after Levi called your father, we changed your flight."

"But, if no one knew about the side trip to Denver and just assumed I was coming straight home, I'd have been here when this happened." Her voice rose at the end to almost a shriek.

Stone nodded. "If you're thinking that somebody from London might've known and then set this off, I don't think so."

She stared at him. "Somebody had to know I was coming home." She shook her head. "That's just too bizarre. The timing's too tight. It's just too much to expect that somebody would've been logging on and searching the airline passenger list, deciding whether I'd be here, and then when I'm not, they tear my house apart," she said. "Or did they think I had come home and then left again?"

Stone froze. "Maybe they did think you would be here. And maybe they also thought you would be bringing something home with you."

She spun around and stared at him in shock. "Oh, my God! The drugs?"

"If it's drugs that were actually seized in England." He pulled out his phone. "I think we better ask Levi to check that out a little closer."

Chapter 10

LISSA SAT INSIDE the Jeep once again. With her arms wrapped tightly around her chest, she tried to find some logical explanation for what had happened to her place. All she could come up with was vandals out having a "fun" night. And that was a terrible thought. But the alternative was so much worse … to think someone was waiting for her to come home … and specifically targeting her.

Stone stood outside the Jeep, talking on the phone. She didn't bother listening. He'd been on the phone for at least fifteen minutes. The conversation seemed to be doing a roundabout. He'd obviously caught Levi before he got into bed, and the two of them were hashing out the same old thing from different angles. Finally the driver side door opened, and Stone sat down behind the wheel.

She didn't know what kind of a solution he would find; she just hoped he had found one. She wasn't ignorant of the fact that this was really her problem. But, if connected to the overseas mess, maybe he'd stick around a little longer and help her out. She'd pushed the bonds of a few days' friendship already way too far.

He turned on the engine and put the Jeep into reverse.

"Where are we going?"

"You're heading to my place, the team's place," he corrected. "We all need some sleep, and then tomorrow we can all sit down and sort this out."

She looked at the road ahead, twisting to take one last look at her property. It might look pretty on the outside, but something was rotten on the inside. She no longer wanted anything to do with it. "Shouldn't we call the police?"

"We will do that in the morning."

She had to be satisfied with that. She was too tired for much else. A tremor ran through her, she felt almost a disconnect from everything going on. Why was this not over? All she'd wanted to do was go home. Instead, it wasn't even habitable. "I'll have to call the insurance company."

"Yes, you will. But again, tomorrow. Let's get through tonight, rest, and recharge. In the morning we'll figure this out."

But just because he said it didn't mean her mind would shut down. Had somebody expected her to bring something back? Had they torn her place apart looking for it? But since she hadn't brought anything, if she'd been home last night, chances were it wouldn't have worked out so well for her. Although theoretically she understood all that, it just seemed so far-fetched.

If it had happened over in Afghanistan—absolutely. She'd believe anything about those people. She'd been kicked, smacked, and hit. But it had never happened on American soil. She considered her home safe.

She stared down at her clenched fists and forced herself to open them. She'd come home expecting to feel safe, to have forgotten, left behind all the bad stuff. Instead she felt cheated, violated.

She was still running on adrenaline and fear. And with no end in sight. "Do you think anybody was still there? Watching us?" She turned to catch his gaze as he stared at her, a hard look in his eyes.

"Why would you ask that?"

She shrugged. "They went to a lot of trouble. Maybe they were waiting around, watching for me." At her words, a tremor rippled down her body. She stuffed her fist into her mouth to hold back a cry.

He reached across and gently clasped her knee. "Don't even think like that. We didn't see anybody. The place was empty."

"But was it really? We didn't look inside the closets. We didn't look under the destroyed bed, what they left of it. It would make sense that they wouldn't jump me if they saw you there." She waved her hand at his body. "You're the size of a bloody tank. Unless they had weapons, they wouldn't want to take you on." She studied his face and added, "And thank you, by the way."

He gave a strangled exclamation. "What are you talking about? Why are you thanking me?"

"I'm thanking you for bringing me home. Because I can't imagine if I'd gone into that nightmare on my own."

He held out his hand, palm up, and just waited. She didn't hesitate. She slipped her hand into his and squeezed his long fingers tight. "I just can't get it out of my head. What if I had come home and interrupted them?" She began to cry.

He squeezed her hand gently. "It didn't happen. It won't."

He dropped her hand to shift gears and took a corner on the road. Thankfully, they were deserted. She was pretty damn sure he wasn't going anywhere close to the speed limit.

"This is the kind of work you do all the time? How do you sleep at night? After your injuries, weren't you always afraid of it happening again? Didn't you wake up in the middle night screaming with the instant replay happening over and over again?"

He nodded. "Absolutely. It's like a nightmare that never ends. But eventually it eases. The power of it diminishes. Sometimes you're really lucky, and it doesn't come at all."

She realized she had unnerved him. She reached across and gently patted his thigh. "I'm sorry. I didn't mean to bring back bad memories."

He laughed. "Don't worry about me."

She studied him. There was an aspect of his personality he hadn't shared, and he likely wasn't ready to. Maybe because she was a female. Giving in to her feelings was a lot easier. She turned to him and said, "Do you ever just surrender? To feelings of fear, of the emotions?"

"Never." His tone was hard and clipped.

She snuggled closer to the door, giving him a little more space. She hadn't meant to pry, didn't mean to prod, but it seemed inevitable. "I'm sorry," she said in a small voice. "It's none of my business. I didn't mean to open old wounds."

"You worry too much."

She didn't. But she wouldn't say another word. It was the least she could do for him. They drove silently for another forty-five minutes. She lost track of the turns he made, even the direction they traveled. She realized just how much trust she'd put in him. He brought her safely out of that horrific terrorist's home in Afghanistan, and now, here in Texas, he was still looking after her. They finally drove into a very large compound. The gates closing behind the Jeep caused her to jump. She couldn't quite hold back her gasp of surprise.

"Don't worry about it. It's not locking us in. It's locking

the world out."

He turned off the Jeep and hopped down. She opened her door and slid to the ground. A huge home with turrets stood before them with more buildings on both sides. She didn't know what to think. As he walked around the Jeep toward her, she said, "What kind of a place is this? It's huge."

"It's home." To him it was that simple.

She'd either get used to it or she wouldn't, but she'd long lost the opportunity to escape. No way was she scaling the gate and fences around her. Then she realized she didn't have to. He stood there with his hand out, waiting, always giving her a chance to say no, or to trust. She put her hand in his once again and said, "Well, I've trusted you so far."

He tucked her hand into his and headed toward one of the doors. As they stepped on a rubber mat, the double doors opened up, and he led her inside.

SHE'D BEEN THROUGH a lot. He would have understood if she'd refused to come into the compound. But he had driven straight in and closed the gates behind them. At this point, he was too damn tired to give an explanation. They were here; they were safe, and the rest of it could be dealt with tomorrow.

But he had to get her inside and set up in a bedroom first. He hoped someone had designated one for her. This house had lots of rooms, some stupid amount, like thirty-two of them. But they weren't all ready and set up with furniture and beds. He'd move her into his bed again tonight if need be. But it would be different in this location.

Still, if that was what was required, then that was what he'd do. She snuggled close as they entered. He couldn't blame her. She didn't know who she could trust. As long as she trusted him, they'd be fine.

Throwing his arm around her shoulders, he didn't give her any option but to keep moving at his pace. He kept going, straight to the stairs. He could've taken the elevator but that would probably be a bit much for her to handle at the moment. The stairs were close. Besides, he remembered her in the truck gasping for air. Claustrophobic.

He led her up the first flight, then the second. His bedroom was the second door, and one of the spare rooms was beside his. The others were on the same floor but down the other wings. At the spare room he opened it up and hit the lights, thankful a made-up bed was ready for her.

"This is yours for the night." He motioned toward the bathroom on the right side of the room and saw a set a towels sitting on the bed. "I suggest you get some sleep, and we'll talk in the morning." He turned to leave, hating the fatigue dragging him down.

One of the things he wanted to do right now was kick that prosthesis across the far side of the room and ease the load on the stump. He knew it would be inflamed. He'd been on it too much. Just as he reached the doorway, he heard her cry out, "Wait."

He spun to look at her. "What's the matter?"

She whispered, "Could you show me where you're sleeping so I know I'm not totally alone?"

He curled a finger and waited until she walked over to him before he said, "This is your door and"—he pointed at the number sixteen, then to the door next to hers with the number seventeen on it—"that's my door."

He walked over and pushed it open, turned on the light, and said, "It's almost a mirror image, and that's where I'm sleeping." He nudged her into her room and pulled the door almost closed. "Get some sleep. Everything will look much better in the morning."

He tugged the door closed. He called out, "Good night," then walked into his room and closed his door firmly. He knew that she'd hear the *click*.

He was too damn tired for anything other than walking over to the bed and stripping down. There he removed his prosthetic leg and laid it down on the floor beside the bed and crashed heavily on the covers. The throbbing in his leg slowly eased. He knew he should put cream on it tonight, but he was too damn tired. The one thing he did do was take a couple muscle relaxants. That was about the extent of what he could handle. And now he hoped he could actually crash.

Everything hurt. He rolled over, closed his eyes, and tried to fall asleep.

Just as he started to fade, he remembered her words. Surrender? Hell, no. He wasn't even sure he knew what that meant. And then he drifted off to sleep.

The door opening woke him up a few minutes later. He bolted upright, and then he knew. "Lissa?"

The door opened wider, and she peered around the corner. He would not be sleeping alone tonight. Internally he was glad. It was important that she be the one to make the decision. He reached across to the inside of his bed and pulled the covers over toward him.

She slipped inside his room quietly, clicked the door closed, and then ran to his bed. She tucked up underneath his sheets and whispered, "Thank you."

He shuffled slightly so he could wrap an arm around her and pulled her up against his big chest. "You're welcome. Now go to sleep."

And just like the last time, she drifted off like a baby. And just like before, he had a hard time.

How was he supposed to sleep with an angel in his arms? Even exhausted, the last remnants of fear still clinging to her, she smelled wonderful. And she felt even better. Lean, long, she fit him like a charm. But the sense of fragility no longer surrounded her.

And that was a good thing. He avoided tiny women. He was a big guy and had always been afraid of hurting them. She wasn't tiny, but she was damn slim.

Still he'd seen her inner spirit, strength, and determination that she had used to get through these last two days. He smiled and pulled her close, whispering, "What am I going to do with you?" And when she answered, he thought he must've heard it wrong because he knew she was asleep. He'd heard her snore gently for a few moments.

She'd been asleep; he'd been sure of it. But he'd also have sworn he heard her say, "Love me. Just love me."

Pleased at the idea, but knowing she was dreaming, he closed his eyes and drifted toward sleep. He took that thought with him. Was love even possible? What he held in his arms right now was just so damn special, he'd do anything to not lose it.

Maybe dreams did come true. He'd never been a dreaming kind of guy, and lately he'd had only nightmares in his world, but maybe, just maybe that was changing.

Chapter 11

LISSA WOKE WITH a start. She lay still, figuring out what was wrong. Or maybe what was seriously right. A man's arms were wrapped around her, holding her close. By just the size of him alone, she knew it had to be Stone. She could feel the soft rise and fall of his chest behind her, the gust of warm breath as it wafted somewhere in the vicinity of her head. She smiled and snuggled closer.

With her eyes closed, she just enjoyed the sensation of being held in someone's embrace. It had been a long time since she'd had a serious relationship. She'd had a few short-term flings in the meantime, but nothing that counted. And overseas she had always been too afraid of the rules of foreign countries to get involved.

Now there was Stone. She never wanted to leave. But this was his home, his space.

Which reminded her of her home, or rather what was left of it. The windows alone could be several thousand dollars to fix. The doors, all the furnishings inside, those were definitely an insurance claim. Almost everything had to be replaced, she knew, and it would be a big job.

She couldn't live there anytime soon. She hadn't for a long time, which meant she must find another place.

She needed to call Marge and let her know. Lissa didn't want her friend and neighbor to show up unexpectedly and see the house like it was.

Add that to the other list of things to do. Plus she had to get a phone—to call the police, the insurance company, and her friend. All of this was a bitter note to herself.

Yet instinct was saying, *Don't move. Enjoy the moment with Stone. Reality will interfere soon enough.* Her exposed shoulders were slightly chilled. She reached up and tugged the covers higher and snuggled a little deeper underneath. She loved the wash of warm air as the blankets closed around her. Somehow she'd caught a bit of a chill with all the traveling. She didn't feel sick—just not quite 100 percent.

"You okay?"

The deep slumber of his voice rolled over her. She patted his forearm wrapped around her chest and said, "Yes. Just cold."

Instantly he shifted her into a deeper embrace, as if he could impart the necessary heat she needed. And, in fact, he could. Just amazing. Like being surrounded by an oven. Being a big man especially, his body was a furnace.

Her eyes drifted closed, and she relaxed. She'd gone to bed too tired to even think about all the events. Now, of course, her mind wouldn't shut off.

Was there a connection between whatever had been put in her luggage and the search of her house? She knew what the answer was. How could there not be? Two strange incidences countries apart and she was the common denominator.

Outside the bedroom door in the hallway she could hear footsteps. She froze. Was somebody likely to come into Stone's bedroom? Would they check out her room and realize she was missing?

She chewed her bottom lip, wondering if she had put

him in a tough spot. And yet, for all that she might, she couldn't feel sorry about where she was right now. For she had been somewhat afraid to be in that room across the hall, a strange bed in a strange bedroom in a strange house. Arriving the way they had, as the minutes ticked by, her fears had gotten worse. And she'd been too tired to work her way through it, so she just came right to Stone. Like a homing pigeon.

"Relax."

His hand reached down and grabbed hers, making her realize she'd been gently petting his forearm.

When he murmured to her, she smiled. Who'd have thought this guy could be ticklish. She pivoted gently in his arms until she was across his chest, her head tucked up on his shoulder. She let her arm drape across his body. He shifted to give her more room, then wrapped his arms around her again. Perfect.

She dropped a kiss on his chest. It just seemed the right thing to do at the time. Besides, if this led to something so much more, she was totally okay with that. Like she'd said, it had been a long time.

To that end, she pushed herself up on her elbow and looked down at him. In the early morning light, he stared at her. A question was in his eyes. She gave him an impish smile and said in response, "Do we have time?"

He slipped a hand up her ribs and along her shoulder, his big thumb reaching to stroke across her cheeks.

But the frown forming in his expression had her narrowing her gaze at him, and she said, "Don't even begin to ask me if I'm sure I want this."

Reaching up to cup his cheek and chin, she slid her fingertips across his lips, and he kissed the tip of one finger. She smiled. "Of all the things I have been through these last few days," she said, "this is the only one that feels right."

And she lowered her head and kissed him gently, just a light exploratory taste.

She draped herself across him, dropping several tiny little kisses on his nose, cheeks, chin, then to his lips. This time she slipped her tongue between his and kissed him for real. There was just something about him she couldn't get enough of. This wasn't her normal behavior, the last two days either. Now that she tasted him, well, she just couldn't get enough.

Stone reached up with both hands, and before she realized what was happening, she'd been rolled over to lie flat on her back.

"There might be time," he whispered.

His lips trailed across her cheeks, warm air from his breathing washed over her. She shivered as tremors rippled down her body. She stretched and laughed, wrapping her arms around his neck.

"But I have no intention of taking a shortcut regardless," he whispered.

He lowered his head and kissed her—a deep, drugging one that seemed to pull at the muscles at the heart of her. She moaned and held him close. When she felt his erection against her, she shifted enough so she could press her pelvis up tight and cuddle him closer. She felt his gasp, but she'd covered his lips with her own, inhaling it, taking and accepting it, and giving it back to him in yet another kiss. He slid his hands down to come up underneath her T-shirt and cupped her breasts.

She made a small cry and arched her back, pressing her breasts into his hands. Her shirt disappeared somehow, and the blankets were pushed away. She could feel the cool air, but she didn't care because her body burned for more.

When he lowered his head and suckled her nipple, taking it deep into his mouth, she twisted and cried out, "Stone, dear God."

He murmured something she couldn't hear but didn't care. His hands, fingers, and mouth were busy caressing, stroking, and tending to the fire within. No embers, but a pure flash fire of heat. Stone. She wanted him. She wanted this. She tried to tug him over her, but he wasn't moving.

Instead he lowered his head straight down to her hip bones, her pelvis. She sat up and tried to tug him higher to kiss him, but it was like trying to move a mountain. When he slid two fingers between her legs, she fell back, crying out, her hips arching up.

She was already wet, waiting, and hot.

He retreated, then slid one finger inside, and she whimpered. "Please, please."

He slipped in a second finger and she realized he was making sure there was room.

She gave a broken laugh. "I won't break."

He lifted his head. Trailing a path with kisses up to her breast, he stopped to feast for a second while his fingers gently teased her. She shuddered, mindless at the gentleness of his hands.

"You sure?" And then he kissed her, his tongue diving deep inside her mouth as he moved on top of her.

When he pushed inside, she wondered if he really was too big. The man was massive, but she didn't expect that part of him to be any larger than normal. She held her breath, and he plunged deep.

She moaned half in pain, half in joy. She wasn't just filled, more like almost being impaled. And yet it felt so damn good. How could anything like this be wrong? And yet she couldn't move as he held her in place.

His arms wrapped around her body, holding her against him. His arms kept her where he wanted her. She tried to stretch, to move, but she really had no place to go.

He tilted her chin and dropped a kiss on her lips. "Still okay?"

She gave a slow, sexy smile, then said, "I am for the moment. If you don't start moving soon, you won't be."

He gave a soft laugh and slowly withdrew, then plunged again. With each one, she was rocked slightly in the bed, and as he withdrew, she cried out, afraid he'd take off and leave her. With his hands holding her hips firm, he drove them both forward.

She twisted, higher and higher, twisting, crying, finally she was pleading, "Stone, please finish this."

He bent over her, raising himself up slightly, holding her head with his hands, his hips moving forward, driving, plunging, taking them toward the end they both wanted.

Her climax ripped through her.

She shook and trembled beneath him. A growl tore free of his throat as his body shuddered over her; something she'd never heard from any other man before. She held Stone close until finally he collapsed beside her, still shaking. After a long moment he wrapped his arms around her and tucked her up close.

This was not what she'd expected, but dammit, she'd take all she could get.

She yawned and snuggled close. "Any chance of a couple minutes of sleep?" she asked.

"Sleep. You'll be fine."

She closed her eyes but not before she slid her arms

around him and held him tight. Dear God, she was getting way too attached to this man. Especially now. Just as she drifted off, she heard the same question he had asked the previous night.

"What am I going to do with you?"

And she answered the same way she had before. "Love me. Just love me."

She closed her eyes and slept.

SO HE HADN'T imagined that response. And she hadn't been dreaming ... Stone couldn't quite believe this woman in his arms—so accepting, gracious, and caring—was here with him. He didn't want to be a hero to her, but he'd known ever since she had first tucked up close to him, that she'd stick by him like glue. He'd wanted her to be able to sleep last night and had been surprised, but also secretly overjoyed, when she'd come to him, again and again. Nice to know that somebody actually cared for him. Sometimes he felt like he was doomed to be alone. But, when he had turned to look at her this morning, she was right here, waiting for him. In more ways than one.

He let his hands slide down her back as he considered the complications.

And there were several.

First, he wasn't exactly ready for a relationship. Not that he was against it; he just hadn't expected to meet a woman anytime soon and even if he did, he figured the artificial leg would be a deterrent. He also realized that she had never asked about it and as yet, hadn't seen the ugly scarring or what he actually looked like when he stood up on just one leg. He knew that would be a shock. Hell, it still was for him every day.

He'd been told by a lot of people that some women just wouldn't care. He was willing to believe that. He just wasn't to believe that would be the case with Lissa. She'd been raised among the wealthy; she'd had the best of everything. Maybe not a great family but she certainly hadn't suffered on a monetary level. She was used to getting her own way and doing what she wanted. That was evident by her turning up her nose to her father at every turn. She showed no fear of reprisals or accountability. And that last one bothered him a lot. He hadn't expected her to end up in his bed, and he could almost hear the others telling him, "Stone, hell, no. Not only is she a case, but she's one that's got some severe complications."

He still didn't understand what had gone on in London. Customs had finally let her go, but he wasn't sure exactly what the issue was. The word "drugs" had been bantered about. He just didn't understand the where, how, or what. Her bag hadn't even been with her. So, therefore, it could've been anybody's actions that led to finding drugs in her bag. And he wasn't even worrying about that part until he had ended up at her house, and then it became an unpleasant reality. What it really meant was … trouble. Something he didn't need in his life right now.

If she was completely innocent, this wasn't something she needed either.

He heard footsteps, followed by the soft tap on his door. When it came again, he knew what the message was. He frowned down at the sleeping beauty in his arms and wondered if he could sneak out without waking her. She should be exhausted. He'd caught six hours of sleep and that would likely be all he got.

That knock had been Rhodes. Stone's presence was required at a meeting downstairs. Soon. Shifting gently, he rolled her on her side, watched until she curled into a ball, covered her up, and then gently eased his weight off the bed. He stood at the side, holding his breath, waiting to see how she'd react.

He needn't have worried; she just snuggled deeper into the covers. He put on his prosthesis first, then quickly dressed. He'd like to shower, but there was just no time. At the doorway he gave her one last glance, realized she was still asleep and likely to be out for hours. He opened the door and slipped out.

He followed the smell of fresh coffee to the kitchen. When he walked in, there was an awkward silence. He ignored it as he headed to the coffeepot and took out his cup. When he turned and studied the table, he realized they all waited for him to say something. He lifted his cup and said, "Good morning."

He kept his voice bland, his face neutral—in no way giving any indication what he'd been doing for the last hour.

Besides, from the look on their faces, they already knew.

Levi walked in just then, stopped when he saw Stone, and said, "Good, you're up. Let's get moving."

Chapter 12

LISSA WOKE UP and realized she was alone and still was too damn tired. She rolled over and curled up to sleep. After the second time, she sat up in the big bed and stretched. She felt so good. Hard to believe she had slept with Stone all night, well, except for a little bit of activity between the sheets. She grinned. And that, of course, had been the best of all. She threw back the covers and slid her legs over the side of the bed.

Standing up, she realized her clothes had been collected nicely at the bottom of it.

As if he'd walked around and gathered her clothes into a pile. That was sweet of him. She shook her head. Who knew clean clothes would be something that she'd crave? Should she stay here or go into the other bedroom? None of her belongings were over there. Hell, she hadn't even gotten undressed in there. She'd lain down on top of that bed and knew she'd never be able to sleep alone.

With that thought in mind, she would stay where she was. She walked into the bathroom, loving the masculine smell of the small room, and stepped under the shower. She'd have to apologize and thank him afterward for letting her use his shampoo because she was desperately in need of getting clean again. She quickly scrubbed down and turned off the water.

When she stepped from the shower with a towel wrapped around her, she heard a noise in the bedroom. She froze.

"Lissa, it's me."

She smiled. "Okay, I'll be out in a second."

She didn't have a toothbrush or hairbrush, but he had a comb on the side of the sink, so she rubbed her hair with the towel, picked up the comb, and quickly tamed her long hair. Then she wove it into a single braid down her back. She flipped it to hang over one shoulder.

Stepping from the bathroom, she joined Stone in the bedroom. He stood beside the window, but the look on his face was not one she'd been hoping to see.

Instantly she apologized. "I'm sorry. I hope it's okay that I used the shower."

She clutched the towel to her chest and wished she was fully dressed already. She collected her pile of clothes and said, "You want me to go to my room?"

"Of course not. Get dressed. I brought you some coffee. We need to talk, and the rest of the team needs to discuss what we'll do from here with you."

Her eyebrows shot up into her hairline. "This involves the rest of them?" She slowly sorted through her clothes as she thought about that. "Just how many people are in the team?"

He laughed. "Just a few more than you've already met. Not to worry." He walked into the bathroom and closed the door. She felt unaccountably pleased to have a few moments of privacy.

She dropped the towel and dressed quickly, figuring he'd given her time on purpose. She'd take the moment as a gift. She wasn't usually self-conscious, but an awkward morning-after scenario was happening here, and she didn't like it. By the time he came out, she was trying to pull her T-shirt down over her still-damp body.

He quickly helped her move the cotton from her sticky skin, unrolling it so it would lie flat. She tossed him a bright smile. "Thank you."

"Don't thank me. If we had been thinking at all, we'd have grabbed you some more clothes last night from your house."

She said glumly, "I considered that this morning myself. It's not that far away, but I can last in these a little longer." She shrugged and picked up the damp towel, went into the bathroom, and hung it up. "I'm sorry. I also used a little bit of your shampoo too," she said self-consciously. "I hope you don't mind. I can always buy you a new bottle."

He laughed and held out his hand. "Stop. It's all good."

"Really?" She studied his face intently, then decided he was being honest. With a beaming smile she reached out for his hand and said, "Thank heavens for that. I was kind of hoping you weren't a stickler for things like that, but … you never know with different people."

"Absolutely you don't know. Come on. Let's get you some breakfast."

She dropped his hand and went to the night table, where she spied the coffee he'd brought her. "I'm not letting the coffee you brought me go cold." She took a deep sip and then moaned with joy. "Is there anything better than waking up to a fresh cup of coffee?"

He walked over, leaned closer, and whispered, "Yes. Waking up to you and hot coffee. Something I didn't get a chance to do this morning."

She could feel the color wash over her face, but smiled at

his compliment.

He reached out and grabbed her hand and said, "Now can we go?"

With her cup only half full, she walked carefully at his side as they exited the bedroom, heading to the hallway. It was the first time she'd actually had a chance to look around.

"This place is huge," she exclaimed. "It's like a fortress."

"Almost," Stone explained. "It is a very safe compound with lots of housing set apart for the unit."

"Unit?"

He turned to look down at her with a smile on his face. "We were all in the military together." He shrugged. "For the four of us who came here and started this originally, it still feels like we're doing the same job."

"If you helped people in the military, then you *are* still," she said, "because you certainly were a huge help to me and the others."

They walked around a corner to another long hallway, where he stopped and pointed to a double-wide staircase. She shook her head. "This place is really grand," she said. "By the way, any update on Kevin and Susan?"

Stone shook his head. "Not yet, but I'm not sure anybody called to get one."

"What about Charles? Has Levi spoken to him yet?" She bounced lightly down the stairs at his side.

She marveled at the big stone construction of the building. Part cement—or maybe stone and cement. She didn't know. But very imposing. The place looked like it had been built to last. And she really appreciated that.

As he came to the bottom of the stairs to another hallway on their right, he motioned for her to carry on in that direction. "You're coming too, aren't you?" She frowned at him. "No way are you leaving me all alone here."

"I wasn't," he said with a smirk. "I was going to tell Levi that you are up."

"No need. I'm here."

Levi's voice washed over her. She spun around to see the big man coming from an office that she hadn't seen on the far side. She gave him a bright smile. "Hi. Thank you so much for letting me stay here last night. Honestly I wouldn't have known where to go or what to do if Stone hadn't been with me."

Levi's gaze lifted and crossed with Stone's. She could feel some kind of hidden communication going on. She didn't want to be *that girl*. She stepped in between them, effectively breaking their eye contact, and said, "Your hospitality is much appreciated. Obviously I'll try to get home and sort out my place as quickly as I can."

He nodded in the direction they were headed. "Come on. Let's get you some more coffee and breakfast. We need to discuss what happened at your place."

She walked into the kitchen with them, shocked when half a dozen men got to their feet, several nodding their heads. "Good morning, ma'am."

She winced at the *ma'am* part. "For those of you who don't remember or didn't know, my name is Lissa. Nice to see you again."

She sat down where Stone motioned and studied the plates in front of the others. She didn't know if they had a chef, but if she could get a plate like they had for herself, she would be very grateful. It seemed like forever since she'd eaten.

Charles had fed them in England, and they'd eaten on the plane, but that'd been because she'd needed the food, not because she'd enjoyed it. This looked like food she could enjoy.

Another man walked into the dining room, a stranger—older, distinguished, and in some ways he reminded her of Charles. He looked at her and smiled. "I'm Alfred. You must be Lissa." He added, "Do you want tea and toast or would you prefer a plate, like the boys?"

She grinned. "If possible, I'd love a plate."

"Good. Be back in a minute."

At that she settled down and realized that somebody had refilled her coffee cup. She turned to glance around and saw Stone replacing the coffeepot on the machine sitting on a sideboard. She grinned at him as he turned to face her. "Thanks, Stone."

He sat down beside her without a word, ever that strong, silent, supportive presence.

The silence around the table grew awkward.

She sat quietly and sipped her coffee, not knowing what to say. Finally, Alfred returned with the plate of twisted sausages and hash browns. "Thank you, Alfred," she said warmly. "This looks wonderful."

And then, completely ignoring the rest of the men, she picked up her knife and fork and dug in. The food was so good. She was starving.

When she plowed through the plate without slowing down, Stone chuckled at her side. "I had no idea you were that hungry."

She cast him a sideways glance and said, "Superhigh metabolism. Can't keep any weight on, and I eat a lot." She picked up a particularly decent-size bite of potatoes and sausage and popped them into her mouth.

Stone said, "Interesting. You don't have either of your

parents' physical traits."

"You noticed that, did you?" She swallowed the rest of the bite and added, "Growing up, I wondered if I even belonged to them. But ... alas I do."

"You know that for sure?" Stone asked, a frown on his face and his tone darkening.

"Yes," she said. "My father insisted on a DNA test when I was born." She grinned at the unusual silence. "Much to his disgust, I'm his." The silence continued. She laughed. "Don't worry about it. At least he knows, as do I." She shrugged as if to say, *What can you do?* She polished off the rest of the food on her plate and sat back with a sigh of satisfaction. "Oh, my God, if you guys ever decide you don't need Alfred ..."

"Fat chance," Stone said with a grin. "And you're not the first one to try to steal him from us."

"I wouldn't steal him, maybe just borrow him for a day or two." She rubbed her tummy and pushed her plate away slightly. "If everybody's done eating," she whispered to Stone, "I'll do the dishes."

Before she even got the words out, Alfred arrived and collected all the plates and cutlery. Stone laughed. "Sometimes he asks for help. The rest of the time he's got it in hand. A commercial-size dishwasher is in there, so usually he's fine."

She nodded and picked up her coffee cup. She expected the discussion about her situation to start soon. She looked at Levi and decided to open it herself. "So, now that I have a full tummy, what was the conversation you wanted to get into this morning?"

He studied her over the rim of his cup. "We've circled back to the theory somebody broke into your house last night looking for what they had smuggled in your backpack, hoping you would bring it into the country."

She froze, slowly lowering her coffee cup. "Right, we're back to that." She turned to face Stone. "It would make so much sense."

"It would, in a way, explain how they knew whatever was in your backpack *was* there," he said. "Because, of course, they were the ones to do it."

She frowned as she worked her way through that. "That would imply they actually knew who I was and were aware I was coming home." She turned her gaze to Levi. "How is that possible? Unless they found out while we were in England?"

"That's what we wanted to ask. How many people knew where you lived? How many did you work with in the refugee camp? Did you get to know any of them well enough to discuss your home life, and would they have had access to your bags?"

She shook her head. "Lots knew I lived in Texas, but few knew exactly where." Her gaze drifted from one stern male face to the next. Where was Ice? Then again it was a huge place, she could be anywhere. Lissa said, "I mean, my bags were always in my room. There wasn't anything you could call a lock on the door. We had a safe where we kept our passports and wallets with our IDs and cash," she added. "But how very presumptuous for people to think I'd be able to bring something back into the country and then for them to come get it from me." She locked her gaze with Levi's. "Besides, didn't they say 'drugs?'"

Levi nodded. "Yes, but a rare form of opium. The British are analyzing it right now in their lab."

Her eyebrows shot up. "Opium? How much was there?"

Levi shrugged. "Enough worth getting out of the country."

"Jesus," she whispered.

TRY AS HE might, Stone couldn't hear any sign of deception in her voice. And he had spent plenty of time learning all the ways people could hide a lie. He was generally a very good judge of character, but he knew he was off his game with her. Nothing like sleeping with a woman to affect your perceptions. And, if she was hiding something, coming to his bed last night would just have been another good way to throw everything off. He hated even thinking that way but hard not to under these circumstances. He glanced at Levi, whose one eyebrow was slightly elevated.

Levi shook his head, a tiny perceptible movement, confirming that he hadn't heard or seen anything either.

That made Stone feel better. As much fun as last night and this morning had been, he'd hate to think he'd been hoodwinked as part of a plan. But she wasn't off the hook yet.

"So what do we do now?" Lissa asked. Her voice trembled, and she'd shifted ever-so-slightly on the bench seat, moving closer to Stone. Her hands wrapped on her coffee cup trembled slightly. Those types of reactions were hard to fake.

Words were one thing, but the physical reactions didn't lie. Also very hard to train someone to produce fake body language.

"Make sure your home is safe and that whoever seems to be following you doesn't return," Levi said.

"And why would he?" she cried out in shock. "Surely, if

he didn't find what he was looking for, he wouldn't come back."

Stone hated to say it, but she needed to understand the danger. "Because he might come looking for you to get the answers he wants."

She turned her head slowly to stare at him, her body slumping. "I don't have any for him. How could I possibly convince anybody I don't know anything about something when I don't know anything about it?" Her voice rose at the end. She reached up a shaky hand and rubbed her temple. "I hate to say it, but maybe I should stay with my parents."

"That might work temporarily, or he might decide to follow you there," Levi said in his no-nonsense tone.

All the color drained from her face. "I can't put them in danger. They didn't do anything to deserve this."

Harrison spoke from across the table. "Did you?"

Stone could see the confusion in her eyes before she turned to stare at Harrison and asked, "Did I do what?

"Do you deserve this?"

She shook her head slowly. "No, of course not. I didn't do this. I didn't do anything. I went over there to help people, to get away from my family. I thought I was doing something useful. And then it all blew up."

"Right." Levi stood up. "You"—he pointed at Lissa—"Stone, Harrison, and I will head to your house now. You can collect a bag of necessities and come back here and stay with us for a few days. I'll call the police. Get this in motion. They will need to make a full report, might check for fingerprints, but I doubt they'd find any—other than yours and Stone's at this point."

"I wore gloves," Stone said.

She stood up. "Thank you," she said sincerely. "I appreciate that. Why wouldn't there be any fingerprints?"

Stone answered for Levi. "Because it was too professional a job. They wouldn't have left fingerprints behind. That's a rookie mistake."

She turned to stare at him. "Professional?" She shuddered. "We're not talking assassins or mercenaries or anything like that, are we?"

"We have no idea what we're dealing with. So let's not jump to any conclusions," Levi said, walking toward the kitchen entrance. "Let's find out the facts first."

With a long face she said, "I'd love to find the facts. So far I don't know anything."

Stone reached up and patted her shoulder. He was delighted—internally—at the idea of her staying with them for a few more days. He'd had worse assignments; keeping a close eye on her had a lot of perks. He just wished they could clear her of all wrongdoings. Then he could really enjoy being with her. It wouldn't feel like he'd crossed the line. Levi hadn't said anything, but Stone knew what Levi was thinking—what they were all thinking.

Stone wanted to believe she was who she portrayed herself to be. But, after being betrayed once, trust was a little harder for the team to give. Stone didn't know what she'd get from this by lying, so, for the moment, he'd give her the benefit of the doubt—and watch his back.

Chapter 13

T HE DRIVE BACK to her house was faster this time. In fact, in daylight, it was a fascinating trip. She'd never been to this corner of Texas before. The compound seemed to encompass a small valley with ridges around two sides of it. As they drove out, the big gates locked and secured the property behind them.

She wondered at their need to always have the gates closed. She turned to Stone and asked, "Have you been attacked in there or something? I just wondered why you keep it locked, especially during the daytime."

"We have actually," he admitted. "But hopefully not again." He turned to look out the window. "And we don't always keep it locked up."

End of conversation. *Right*. She stayed quiet for the rest of the trip until they hit the small town where her home was. As they drove into the cul-de-sac and up to her place, she knew the front, which appeared undamaged, hid what was so much worse in the back, especially in the cold, harsh reality of day. Like a facade, it hid the evil that lurked beneath.

And somehow she'd gotten caught up in it.

They exited the truck in silence. She watched as Levi studied her townhome and then every other one on the block. One large row-house complex. Twelve in this unit. She had the end one. Beside her was a fence and then a large playground. She stepped forward and led the way around the rear.

She braced herself but couldn't hold back the gasp, still was shocked to see it again. She stepped out of the way as Levi gave the place a solid once-over from the outside. She had no idea what he thought he was looking for.

He obviously noted the busted doors, pushed them open, and stepped inside. She waited for Harrison to join him. Stone, however, wouldn't let her stand outside alone. He motioned for her to follow the other two.

She frowned up at him. "What if I don't want to go in?"

He shrugged. "Then I'll stay out here with you." He turned to look at the busted windows and said, "I thought you wanted to come."

"I did," she said quietly, then admitted, "but that doesn't mean I'm up for going back inside." Before she'd said her last word, he'd held out his hand. Always offering support. Always offering security. She'd do a lot to have a man like this.

She reached out and gripped his fingers, hard. "What if they came back?"

"Chances are, we won't know. They made such a mess the first time," he said with a mocking laugh.

"If they were watching us," she argued, "then they would know if I went inside."

"And, if they are watching you, they would know you brought nothing in. And that we weren't here long enough for you to do very much."

"Good point." Feeling better, she ended up dropping his fingers and walking inside; then she headed straight for the stairs. As she climbed, she realized that the other two men had stopped and watched her silently. She shivered. She really wanted them to believe her. But this was still hanging over her head.

A new feeling for her. She wasn't used to being under suspicion. Well, other than from her father.

At the bedroom doorway she stopped and studied the mess. She couldn't possibly know for sure, like Stone had said, but it didn't appear to be any different than when she'd left in the wee hours of the morning. Only now it looked harsher. In the bright light the damage, the mess, and the work ahead seemed even more depressing.

On the far left side, she spied her large traveling bag. More like a beach bag but with a zipper—so she sometimes used it as a carry-on for a flight. She carefully picked her way through the mess and grabbed the bag. She upended it to make sure it was empty, then walked over to the dresser. She'd been gone a long time and had taken the bare necessities with her. She hadn't even lived in this house for much more than four months before she had left it, so the drawers weren't very full. But she did have a few changes of clothes. She quickly packed up what was in her drawers, then turned to the closet and winced.

Some of the clothing had just been tossed on the floor, but a lot of it appeared to have been ripped. She didn't understand that part. It was more vindictive. Like a woman who hated another. But she honestly couldn't think of any woman who hated her so much. She hadn't cultivated many friends over the last ten years.

She picked through the closet, making a pile of usable clothing. She found a couple cardigans, a simple dress, several blouses, and skirts. If she took the skirts, she would need shoes. She wasn't sure any of those were wearable either.

Stone spoke from behind her. She turned with a pair of sandals she'd forgotten she owned in her hands as he said, "You finding what you need?"

"I'm finding what's left that's still usable. Why would they possibly want to rip my clothing?" She held up an evening dress where the shoulder pads had been opened.

He frowned. "We're back to considering they thought you might've hidden whatever they're looking for."

She stared at the shoulder pads, then back at him. "If that's true, then what they're looking for is damn small."

"We knew that, but we didn't know how small."

As she watched, his gaze wandered to her bag, mostly filled now with the least-damaged clothing left in her bedroom.

"Is that all you have?"

She nodded. "A lot of it has been destroyed, and I didn't have very much to begin with. Plus, I've been traveling." She turned toward the closet and spied an old purse. She crowed with delight. "Oh, perfect." She snagged it, walking carefully through the mess. Taking it over beside her other bag, she dumped the contents of the purse on the bed, delighted to find a little bit of her makeup and a hairbrush. She beamed. "Oh, to know how to appreciate the simple things in life." She picked up the hairbrush, waved it at him. "Now I don't have to borrow your comb anymore."

He shook his head. "Glad you're happy with the simple things."

"Oh, I am."

She gave her bedroom one last walk-through, packing away as much as she could. Scouring through the mess, she found a scarf she'd always loved, and a pair of socks rolled off to the side. She snagged those up too. Then she headed to the bathroom. Some things should be left in there, but, as she walked into the small room, she realized her intruder had been before her here as well. The contents of the cabinets below the sink had been emptied—no longer usable.

"Looks like they opened everything and dumped it on the floor." She stood in the doorway, her expression full of dismay. "I don't understand that mind-set."

Stone made his way behind her and studied the mess. "That will take work to clean up."

She turned to face him, appalled. "My God! Do I have to do all that?"

"Your insurance should take care of it. But we have to get the police report filed first."

As if they'd heard his words, she could hear a vehicle driving up, parking in the driveway. She glanced out the window and saw a cruiser. Two local policemen got out, walking to the front door. She quickly grabbed her bag and made her way down the stairs. She dumped the bag in the front hallway and opened the door. The first man tilted his head at her and said, "Ma'am, we heard there was a break-in."

She made a face. "There are break-ins, and then there is this break-in," she said. "Yes, it's been broken into, but the entire place has been trashed." She stepped back and motioned for them to enter. "Come on in."

They entered, took one look at the living room, and shook their heads. They silently walked through the entire house. She didn't even follow. What was the point? Stone had stayed at the top of the stairs, and she saw Levi and Harrison leaning against the hallway wall, watching the uniformed guys quietly. The new arrivals just nodded at the other men.

She wondered at the lack of friendliness on all five male faces. Was that standard or just something very male? She walked to the library, wondering if anything else could be salvaged, but there was really nothing. The room was cold and empty. She checked the downstairs bathroom and then went into the kitchen. She'd hardly even cooked here. Everything was of decent quality, but nothing held memories that she wanted to hang on to. Systematically she went through the cupboards to see if she'd forgotten anything. She opened one cabinet and found her keys. Pulling them out, she stared down at one of them.

"What do they open?" Stone asked at her side.

"This is my spare house key. This is my spare car key. I parked my car at Marge's place. Why would I want to leave it here all the time without anybody living here?" She pulled up the other key and frowned. "I think this is my safety deposit box key, but I'm not sure why it would be here."

"Where else would it be?"

"In my purse." She turned to study the rest of the room.

"Except that you left the country for eight months, so would you have taken it with you? Why not leave it here with all the rest?"

"That's sensible. And it's likely what I did. I don't remember exactly. Such a long time ago."

She pocketed all the keys and continued to rummage through the kitchen. But it was virtually empty. At the entryway closet she opened the door, happy to see two of her jackets still there, apparently not cut or destroyed in any way. She slipped one over her shoulders and the other she packed in her bag. She picked up her purse and plopped her keys into it.

Turning to Stone, she said, "Any chance of a trip to the

bank so I can get money and new bank cards?"

He nodded. "We can do that. But we have to deal with the police first."

"Right." She turned to the policemen who were now in the living room and asked, "What do I need to do?"

"Come on down to the station and file a report."

The second man, who'd been quiet so far, looked at her and said, "Do you have insurance?"

She nodded. "I haven't been home for eight months because I traveled to Afghanistan. I set up special insurance just for that reason."

"Good. They won't be very happy with you."

She winced. Between the broken windows, damaged floors, contents strewn about, this would be a pretty big bill. On the other hand, it wouldn't be hers. That worked for her.

Her parents may be megarich, but she wasn't; yet she was well-off. Enough to ride through this mess if she had to.

WHILE LISSA CHATTED with the two cops, Stone headed over to the guys. It had been interesting to watch what she considered worth saving. She had collected clothing and a few articles from the bathroom but not much. Yet she'd been delighted when her old purse had yielded a bit of makeup. She picked up no valuables. She collected no mementos. In the kitchen, she collected her keys, but that was it. Straightforward, no-nonsense, common sense woman. He liked it.

And he liked her.

He walked over to Levi and said, "Let's take her to the police station so she can get that process started. Then we'll go to the bank so she can get money and new bank cards."

She had mentioned she'd stored her vehicle at a friend's.

He glanced around the room and asked, "The same friend who's been keeping an eye on the place has your car?" Stone asked Lissa loudly. When she nodded, he added, "While we're here, we'll need to talk with her and see what we can find out."

Lissa added, "She doesn't live in my complex, but she's not far."

Levi's phone rang just then. Stone waited patiently after he heard the name Kevin. He watched as his friend's face hardened. Harrison walked closer, sensing something going on. When Levi got off the phone, he pocketed it and said, "Kevin's gone missing."

The three men exchanged a hard look. "Missing, as in possibly dead, or as in he slipped out of the country?" Harrison asked.

Levi's glare deepened. "Either or both. No one knows anything at the moment."

"And Susan?" Stone asked.

Levi shrugged. "That's likely the reason he's gone AWOL. She passed away last night."

"What? I thought she was just worn out." Stone hated to hear that. Sure she'd been tired and not looking very good, but he didn't think she had been that bad. But once she'd been hospitalized, the team had lost touch as to the updates. He'd have to tell Lissa; the news would be upsetting.

Harrison brought up a point that Stone had completely overlooked. "When did he go missing?" Harrison asked in a slow, drawling voice. "Interesting that he does and Lissa's place is broken into. Because Kevin could easily have been smuggling something into the country and using her as his mule."

The three men stood in silence, contemplating the possibility.

"Interesting thought," said Levi. "We'll keep it in mind. The question is, after Kevin's wife died, what happened to him and his plans?"

"And that's the problem. It's supposition. We have no way to know. Too many plausible explanations here." Harrison headed toward the back door. "We need to find out the truth."

As they walked toward the vehicle, Levi's phone rang again. He glanced down at the number and frowned. Then he walked several steps away from everybody and answered it.

Lissa walked up behind Stone. They were both just far enough away that they couldn't hear Levi's conversation.

"What's the matter?" she asked him.

"I'm not sure."

Whoever Levi was talking to was really pissing him off. His back was rigid, and his free hand was clenched into a fist before he shoved it into his pocket. Finally Levi put away his phone and stood for a long moment before walking off into the distance. Then he spun on his heels and said, "Lissa, that was your father."

She cringed instinctively, her hand grabbing Stone's. Then she straightened, lifted her chin, and said, "What did he want?"

"His bonus back."

She gasped. "That's not fair. You had nothing to do with me leaving."

"Your father seems to feel we did," he said in a laconic tone. "Even though you didn't get into the limo at the same time we did, and he saw you go upstairs. However, the driver would've known exactly who took you to the airport."

She glared at him. "Let me borrow your phone so I can

talk to him."

"No, that's not happening. You want to pick a fight with your father, you do it on your time and your phone." And he turned and walked over to the truck to get in.

She swallowed hard. Stone grinned down at her. "Don't worry about it. That's between Levi and your father. Levi's too cagey to let it go down like this."

"Maybe. But I don't want him to lose out because of me," she said forcefully. "My father wouldn't even miss that little bit of change he handed out. And you guys have been so helpful that I feel like I should be paying you for this, but I don't have any money at the moment." She stopped and looked at Stone. "Am I paying you for this?"

"You're not. I'll talk to Levi and see what the deal is. But, if he didn't mention anything upfront, he certainly wouldn't be charging you on the sly. Levi's too honorable for anything less." Stone motioned toward the truck. "Get in."

She hopped in. Both Levi and Harrison were in the front; she and Stone were in the back again. "I'm sorry, Levi. My father can be very difficult."

"Well, he's about to learn I can be too. Somebody set you up. And, like I told him, for all I know he's the one who did it."

Stone laughed. "I bet he backed off on threatening to pull the bonus check after that."

"He didn't back off much. But, from his reaction, I don't think he was involved. He's also horrified to think that his daughter is involved in some kind of smuggling operation."

Stone watched Lissa slump into the corner.

"But I'm not," she said defiantly. "I have nothing to do with this."

"Then let's find a way to prove it."

Chapter 14

F OR A DAY that had kicked off pretty damn decently in Stone's bed, it was rapidly going downhill. Still she made it through the filing of the report at the station, then, at the bank, she got money and ordered replacement cards. She was also relieved to see that no unexplained withdrawals had showed up on her bank account, at least as far she could tell.

After all, if somebody had gone through her house, maybe they'd also wanted her money. But, with that out of the way, she had to admit to feeling much better.

Once again outside, the men leaning against the truck, she realized what she really needed was to get her wheels again.

She stood in front of them and asked, "If I could ask for one more favor … could I get a ride to my friend's house where I can pick up my car?" She pulled her car keys from her purse and said, "That way I can be mobile again. You wouldn't have to run me all over the place."

The men exchanged glances, then Levi gave a curt shake of his head. "You have to get insurance on your vehicle so you can drive it again."

"Right." She'd forgotten about that. "I seem to have forgotten the simple basics of living here." She reached up and rubbed her temple. "I'd like to just go home and take a nap.

But …"

She caught the way Stone looked at her, then realized she had no home. She was hopefully still allowed to go to Levi's place …

But they'd done so much for her, she hated to impose. She straightened her back. "Look, I can go to my friend's house and stay there," she said. "I haven't spoken with her yet, as I don't have a phone, but I'm sure it would be okay with her."

"Let's get your phone first," Stone said. "Then we'll run past the house and see about getting your car. Right now you can't make a good decision about what you want to do."

She smiled up at him. "Thank you for being very kind."

He rolled his eyes. "I haven't done anything anyone else wouldn't have done. Come on. Let's get into the truck. Hopefully we can grab a new phone for you someplace."

Once in the vehicle, the discussion was about cell phone plans. As it happened, a phone store was at the end of the block. Levi quickly pulled up, and they walked in. Within twenty minutes she had a new cell phone and a new number.

She grinned, almost doing a happy dance. "I forgot how good it felt to be connected. This last week has been kind of tough," she admitted. "I didn't have Internet most of the time I was over there, and those of us who had cell phones, they didn't work, except for Kevin's. Mine worked for the first bit, but then the battery died, and the charger didn't fit the electric plug-in. The outlet kept shorting and …" She shrugged. "The end result was, my phone was useless for most of the time. I'd check it every once in a while, but … Kevin ended up giving me his old cell after he bought a new phone on one of his trips. Of course it wasn't reliable either. Hence, why he got a new one, but it was something."

"Trips? What kind of trips?" Levi asked.

"It's kind of hard to explain because I really don't know the details," she said. "I was there in a different capacity than they were. I was just there as a volunteer to help out. I didn't get paid, but got room and board. I paid for my own travel. Of course most of the people got reimbursed for their travel costs if they needed it. In Susan's and Kevin's case, because they were both doctors, they were on a medical program. He was coming to Texas soon for a conference, but I guess that's out now."

She frowned. "And they went around helping in other refugee camps. I saw them come and go for a while, and then they were stationed at the same one I was at for the last few months. But still they flew in and out, getting medical supplies and trying to drum up financial support. Maybe just some R&R for them." She shrugged. "I don't really know all the details. Volunteering was a chance to be somebody I wasn't. A chance to let all my history fall away and just help others. I didn't ask questions, and very few people asked any of me."

She stared out the window as the truck rumbled toward her friend's house. "It was a different lifestyle. A chance to step out of the regular world and be someone new."

"And who were you over there?" Stone asked curiously.

She smiled. "I was nobody. Exactly how I wanted it. My father wasn't a senator. My mother wasn't one of the ladies of the clubs. I was just me. I slept on bunk beds, cleaned up in the kitchens, and gave children hugs. I was a volunteer who did anything and everything. Sometimes I did clerical work, assisted in the medical rooms, others I helped in the kitchen." She smiled with the memories. "It didn't matter to me. I was happy to pitch in wherever."

"What kind of training do you have?" Harrison asked. "You said something about boarding school and college."

"Yes. And again my father decreed I become an art major. I actually went into business." She smiled at the surprised look on their faces. "Just because I don't like my father's money doesn't mean I don't like it as a whole." She upped the wattage of her smile. "And I do like to look after money. If nothing else, the business degree gave me the ability to handle what I do have."

"And do you have money?" Harrison asked. "Normally we wouldn't ask that, but considering you were kidnapped, who your father is, and how you are avoiding him ..."

"My grandmother was very wealthy. She left me a trust fund."

Harrison snorted. "Lucky you."

"Actually I can now say you're right. It is lucky me." She turned to gaze at the scene traveling past the windows. "For a long time though I didn't see the value. I do now."

Stone's quiet voice reached her. "Sometimes, through the hardest adversity, we truly understand what's important."

She turned and looked at him, her eyes getting misty. He'd been to hell and back and survived. She could do no less. "I'm not as good a person as you are," she said, "but I'm trying."

His eyebrows shot up in surprise. "What makes you think I'm a good person?"

She laughed. "Stone, I've said it before and will again—you're a gentle giant with a big heart."

HE REALLY SHOULDN'T let her get away with calling him that. It would completely ruin his image. He was a badass, always had been, planned to always be one. But in quiet moments, he would allow that he could be warm and fuzzy inside.

Probably not a good thing. He caught sight of Harrison's grin and realized that, as far as the guys were concerned, that nickname would stick. Okay, so he was gentle and big, and maybe he was packing ten pounds too much, but it was all muscle.

And he'd stand by that any day.

Of course he also dropped thirty pounds when he lost his leg. The doctors had been good to him. And he'd be the first to say it could have been so much worse. He had a few other injuries, but they'd all healed. Physiotherapy had helped. Yet how damned amazingly hard it had been to relearn how to walk when he didn't have a foot. Something so simple and yet so damn precious.

Finally, with all the errands done, they dropped her off at her friend's house. She pointed to the car in the driveway, set off to one side. A small bright-red Prius.

He grinned. Figured she'd pick something like that. Bright but not flashy but definitely a statement. He slid from the truck on his side and waited for her to come around, and together they walked up to the front door. She'd already pulled her keys from her purse and flicked the unlock button at the Prius. Instantly they both heard the locks unlock with a *click*.

"How nice to have wheels again." At the front door she knocked and waited for her friend to answer. But no one came. She pulled out her new phone, added her friend's name, and quickly dialed the number.

He glanced at Levi and Harrison, but they weren't going anywhere. Not until they knew she had either a place to stay or her wheels to follow them to the compound.

She knocked again and held the phone to her ear as she tried to call her friend inside. Stone crossed his arms, wondering if she might be out. He walked around to the side and peered in the living room window. What he saw made his heart freeze. He immediately made a slashing move toward the men in the truck. He grabbed Lissa's hand and dragged her to the truck, ignoring her protests. He shoved her into the backseat and barked, "Stay here."

The others were already out of the truck. They headed around to the rear of the house. Stone went to the front, checked the lock on the door, and realized there wasn't one. He pushed open the door, making sure he was hidden from view. When he heard the signal from the back door, he entered.

He went in low, weapon raised. The living room had been trashed, similar to Lissa's house. But no one was in the house. He quickly made his way to the back room and around to the kitchen. The others were there, standing, staring.

A woman a few years older than Lissa's age was tied to a chair. Blood no longer dripped from her dead body.

She'd been shot in the head. But it didn't look like the killing had happened quickly as evidenced by the blood on her wrists and beaten face. Her feet had been tied to the chair legs, and she looked like she'd been here for a while.

He turned, grim-faced, to the guys and said, "This woman was supposed to have checked on Lissa's house the same day we flew in."

"Are we thinking somebody, while watching the house waiting for Lissa to come home, instead saw this girl?" Harrison turned to study the rest of the kitchen. "And followed her here and beat her up, looking for information?

The poor girl didn't know anything."

"And that's when they shot her," Levi said.

"Oh, my God."

Stone spun to see Lissa standing in the doorway, both hands clasped over her mouth, tears in her eyes as she stared in horror at her friend.

He raced to her side. "Damn, I told you to stay in the truck."

She turned her face toward him, and crumpled into his arms.

He held her close and spoke to the other two. "We need to do a sweep of the house," he said in a low voice. "Just because she's dead doesn't mean they didn't stay here."

Both men disappeared through the doorway. Stone held Lissa close. He rubbed her back and shoulders and dropped a kiss on her forehead beside the stitches. They needed to get those removed soon. "I'm so sorry, sweetheart. I was hoping to save you from seeing this."

She shook her head. "She's dead because of me, isn't she?"

How could he answer that? Probably, yes. And yet Lissa wasn't to blame. He led her through the front door, onto the small porch, and made her sit down on the steps. "Look, you need to stay here. We can't contaminate the scene. We need to make sure whoever did this isn't still here nor will return. I need to trust you. Can you stay here for me?"

He could see the shaking start. But no way could he help her. Right now they had to make sure the place was safe.

He reached out and gently stroked her head. "Lissa?"

"It's okay. I'll be fine," she whispered. "I promise I'll stay here."

With that vow Stone went back into the house and raced upstairs. In the master bedroom he stopped to see it had been completely destroyed. Even worse than Lissa's. Both Levi and Harrison were poking through the mess. "Anything?"

"Not that we can see. It's similar to Lissa's house. Everything destroyed as if they were searching for something. But this room seems to have received particular attention."

He looked around. "It's pretty darn hard to imagine why though. And if they found anything, there's no way to know."

"Considering the disaster here, I'm guessing they didn't."

Harrison kicked a drawer and shrugged. "This just looks like rage again."

They both stared at Stone. "You think she would know anything about the contents of this room?"

"She might, but she's been gone for eight months, so who knows what or how it's changed since then."

"Right."

"We need to call the police again," Stone said. "This could be enough to finish her."

"They'll ask more questions, but that's all," Harrison said. "Where is she staying tonight?"

"She's coming home with us," Levi said. "Til we get to the bottom of this, she needs to stay somewhere safe."

Stone nodded. "I agree, but we also can't forget the fact that we've now shown up at these two locations. If anybody's watching these houses, they may very well be following us to the compound."

"Which is exactly why, as soon as we left this morning, it went on lockdown," Levi said calmly. "Ice is watching. She'll know if anyone is hanging around."

"Good. Let's get this show on the road then. The sooner we're home safe and sound, the better."

Chapter 15

S HE WAS NUMB, just not enough. She could still feel the waves of grief as they roared through her system. This was so not fair. Marge had never done anything to hurt anyone. In fact, she'd been such a good friend to keep an eye out on her place. Lissa understood it was a case of being in the wrong place at the wrong time, but she'd seen what they'd done to her friend. It terrified her. Marge had been a hell of a nice person.

What would these men do to Lissa if they caught her?

Even as she considered that, her body made a small cry of protest. She couldn't think of that right now. First she had to face the police again. This interrogation would be a little deeper, longer, and harder.

But the men stood by her side and explained what was going on. That helped. She couldn't imagine being a woman alone trying to do this. It just looked a whole lot like rage and jealousy from the condition of Marge's bedroom.

Until the police had the autopsy report on Marge, Levi couldn't prove that Lissa was out of the country at the time of Marge's death.

When they could, it'd be a small relief, considering her best friend was dead. She curled up in the front seat as Stone drove her now-insured car. Not a long drive, yet part of her wished it was a much longer one. She just wanted the world to go away. So she could try to forget what had happened. To pretend Marge—that bright, beautiful young woman—was still alive and laughing.

No wonder she hadn't answered her phone. She couldn't.

Lissa didn't want to return to the compound. Everyone around her was dying. She didn't want anyone else to get hurt. She tried to tell Levi to leave her alone, that she was nothing but bad news for his team and home. That whoever had done this to Marge would come after them for helping her.

He held up his hand and said, "Don't ever say that again. From now on, Stone will look after you."

And she'd fallen silent and let Stone lead her around like the lamb she'd become.

Dear God, she hoped her parents didn't find out about this. It would just give her father even more ammunition for years to come. He'd then tell her how she was such a wreck that she was destroying the lives of everybody around her. He'd told her that once before, and it had hurt so badly.

Only now, as she stared down at her long history with her father and this recent event, did she realize maybe he was right. She was always making impulsive decisions—though she thought for the right reasons. But currently, with such a fallout as this, she wondered if maybe he'd been right all along.

"Don't try to think," Stone said quietly in the darkness. "Just relax. It'll take time to get over this."

"I don't think time can help much," she murmured painfully. "She was a really beautiful person."

He reached across and grabbed her fingers, interlacing them with his. "I'm sure she was. So you'll need to grieve for her loss, and then we'll honor her life and find a way to make her passing a little easier on you."

She didn't think such a thing was possible. But she knew people lost someone special all the time. She'd just been blessed to not experience that until now.

It hurt too much.

Instantly a wave of grief washed over her and brought the tears dripping down her cheeks again. Surely no more were left inside? She hadn't cried since forever, barely making it through the police interviews. She was actually afraid they'd ask her to go to the hospital to see somebody, get counseling—and that wasn't happening.

The car slowed unexpectedly. She peered in front of them and realized they were already at the compound. Stone drove her car in and parked around the side, out of sight with the other vehicles, blocking it from view. Levi and Harrison drove up behind them and parked the truck, damn-near blocking the car from moving anywhere.

Her mind was fuzzy. She thought she understood their reasoning but wasn't sure anything mattered anymore. They were trying to protect her, and she was beyond caring. So many people hurt. It should have been her.

Stone got out and came around to open the door for her, helping her to her feet. Instead of trying to push her inside, he just held her close. She burrowed into his arms and clasped her hands behind his back.

She couldn't think of another time in her life that she had had somebody to just hold on to. Someone who was willing to help her through a tough patch in her life. Someone so very special to her.

Also, something she couldn't afford to get used to. They hadn't spoken about anything personal between the two of them. She was in no shape right now to even consider something like a relationship, but she knew she wanted to keep him in her life if at all possible.

She had no idea how she'd fit into something like the ex-military unit living at this compound. They had a good thing here. The only couple appeared to be Levi and Ice, and Lissa didn't know the details behind them either.

Finally she stepped back and gave Stone a watery-eyed smile and said, "Thanks. Any chance I can go lie down?"

He slipped an arm around her shoulders and kept her close. "Good suggestion. Come on. Let's get you into bed. You didn't get a lot of sleep last night and have had nothing but shocks ever since."

Just the thought of nearing a bed was enough to keep her putting one foot in front of the other. She let him lead her where he would. When she realized she was standing beside the same bed she'd awakened in this morning, her heart melted a little bit more. "Are you sure?"

He laid her purse and bag down on the floor beside the night table and turned to look at her, asking, "Am I sure about what?"

She paused before answering. This was his bed, his bedroom. "I kind of pushed the limit by coming in here last night. Are you sure you want me to stay here with you?"

"I thought we were past that stage actually," he said with a smile. "You shouldn't be alone right now. So I'm totally fine with this. But maybe I should be asking if you're okay with it?"

He waited for her to answer.

Inside she was torn up with grief and with all her emotions, it was like she had no filters anymore. She didn't know what to say or how to say it. At first she was afraid it would come out wrong and then realized she just didn't give a damn anymore. She slipped her arms around his shoulders and said, "There's nothing I want more."

She just hugged him and held on tight. She didn't even understand how, but, a few minutes later, she was lifted and placed on the cool sheets, completely naked, with the blankets tucked up over her from her shoulders down. A gentle kiss was dropped on her temple.

But somehow, in her foggy mind, she realized he had made the impossible happen. "You're a miracle, you know that?"

"No," he whispered. "I'm not. I'm just a man."

And he disappeared from the room.

She lay in the half cloudy space that she'd entered and felt the waves rise once again. And she gave into them, letting the tears flow and the sobs ripple through her as she cried herself to sleep.

THEY HAD BIGGER problems now. Stone closed the door quietly behind him, his heart aching at her sobs. But he couldn't help her or hold her right now. He had to let the storm fly through her system and come out the other side, where she could slowly piece her life together again.

It wasn't just the loss of her friend that gave her that guilty feeling but believing she was somehow responsible for the murder of her friend. Because their association *had* likely gotten the young Marge killed. It would be hard to dissuade Lissa from believing she wasn't responsible. That none of this was her fault would take a lot for her to believe right now.

He walked into the kitchen, headed straight for the coffeepot. After pouring himself a big mug, he leaned against the counter, facing the group collected around the table.

"How is she?" Ice asked. "That's got to be a tough shock for her."

"She's crying right now. Should be asleep in minutes." He shrugged and sat down heavily at the table. "She's in shock. Overwhelmed with grief. And horrified that she's responsible for Marge's death."

The others nodded. They understood.

"Anything unusual happening here today, Ice?" Stone asked. "Any sign somebody is watching the place or that we brought anybody here?"

"Not so far." She glanced at Logan. "You've been watching the monitors. Any alerts?"

Logan shook his head. "Not yet. But, if they saw the number of us and the sheer size of the place, I wouldn't expect them to do anything stupid. They might just hang around and check out the place for a while. Lay low and make a plan."

Levi nodded. "But I'm not sure this was as organized and as professional a job as we would've done."

"Why would they murder the woman?" Harrison asked, anger threading through his voice. "And I think the damage to her place was more for show than anything. When they finally believed she didn't know anything about Lissa and didn't have anything of hers, they shot her." He stared down at his coffee cup. "The rest was just for staging."

"Can anybody come up with any other explanation than Lissa being used as a mule to smuggle something across the borders?" Ice asked. "We've certainly seen it happen before. But never with this kind of an end result."

"In this case, she didn't have the bag. If she did, then maybe it warranted this kind of attention but she didn't ..."

Stone said.

"Nothing else makes any sense," Ice added.

"We'll figure it out. But it never seems to make sense until the very end." Levi stood and refilled his coffee cup. "I also spoke to Charles."

The others turned to look at him.

Harrison asked, "What about Kevin?"

"No sign of him." Levi shrugged. "And we still don't know if that's ominous or not. Or maybe he didn't give a shit." He turned to look at Ice. "Although, from what we saw in Afghanistan, he appeared to be a very caring husband. So the other alternative is, he's lying somewhere dead in an alleyway."

Ice winced. "Did Charles do a background check on Kevin and Susan?"

"He's looking into it now. But, so far, nothing's showing up."

"Have you considered that they were the ones doing the smuggling? Or that they were also targeted for smuggling?" Stone asked. "We brought three people back with us. We were only expected to bring one. And we got all three through customs at Heathrow."

"I was wondering about that." Levi sat down on the bench. "But getting information on Kevin and Susan is turning out to be hard to do. Charles is the best man for that job, and he is struggling."

"What do we do from here?" Stone asked.

Levi turned to stare at Harrison. "Okay, well, I think Merk has a few connections with mercenaries, as do you, Harrison. Maybe send out feelers and see if somebody knows anything about the job."

Harrison nodded. "I'll try. This isn't exactly a typical job though."

"I know. I'll also contact a few of our old brass and see if anybody can get a line on what happened at customs," Ice said. "Maybe a little bit more information was being withheld."

Harrison smiled. "Sometimes honey works better than lemons."

Ice stood up and patted Harrison on the shoulder. "I'll do that now. I'll be in the office if anyone needs me."

Stone stood up. "I'll check on Lissa, then see if I can grab some sleep." He stood up and walked to the doorway. He knew the others were watching him. He turned at the last minute and said, "I did check out her car." He stopped and shoved his fingers in his pockets. He pulled out the contents of the glove box and dropped it on the kitchen table. "I don't think any of this means anything, but I haven't had a chance to check. Remember, she's been gone eight months."

"Do we know that for sure? Anyone?" Harrison asked. "Not trying to be a shithead here but, at least, confirm she has been out of country for that long."

"I'll do it," Levi said. "We can find that out pretty damn fast."

Stone nodded. "If you check further, prove she's legit. Because I hate to say it, but I'm falling hard. Make sure I've got a soft place to land, not another nasty betrayal after Rodriguez. I lost a leg to that one. I don't want to lose my heart to her."

With those harsh words he turned and walked out, leaving the men to stare in his wake.

Chapter 16

S HE FELT THE heat soak through her chilled body and bones until it became a burning furnace where she had been added to the hellfires of the damned.

"Easy, Lissa. Stop crying, honey. You'll make yourself sick."

Internally she knew she was already. Something was wrong with her. People didn't love her like they did other people. Something just wasn't right with her world. Why did shit like this keep happening?

But she also realized that the man speaking was Stone, and he was really worried about her. He held her tight against his chest, and that was the source of the furnace. She opened her watery eyes and wiped at her tears, trying to dry them enough to see him through the waterfall. "I'll be fine," she sobbed. "It's just so hard right now."

He dropped his head and kissed her deeply. She wrapped her arms around his neck and whispered, "Make me forget. Just for a moment, help me forget."

He rolled her to her back and positioned himself right between her thighs. Dear God, exactly where she wanted him to be. He kissed, stroked, and caressed her, all while her emotions were jumbled, mixed, and torn. But it wasn't long before she twisted beneath him. When he finally entered her body, she welcomed him with all her heart. She wrapped her legs around his hips as high as she could go, and she hung on for the ride. A journey to remember. He didn't just stop at one climax. He rode her right through and drove her off the cliff again and then again. By the time she lay boneless in his arms, with him sated at her side, she knew she'd died and gone to heaven. For real this time.

"Do you believe in heaven?" she whispered. "I desperately want to believe that Marge is someplace better."

"I believe there is something else beyond us all," he whispered against her ear, rocking her in place. "And you know that she's there. Hold that thought. Believe it."

She smiled because he understood. Even if she didn't for herself, she knew Marge had believed it. She'd been a staunch Protestant, and a firm believer that she would go to heaven. In her heart, Lissa knew if there was a heaven, Marge was knocking on the front door right now and that there'd be no problem letting her friend in. She was one of the good people in the world.

"Now go to sleep." He shifted her body slightly so she could curl up, spooned next to him like the previous night.

And with his arm wrapped around her body, his hand cupping her breast, she snuggled deeper and smiled. "What if I don't want to?" His chuckle rippled through her back, making her body vibrate on the bed. She laughed as she rolled over. "Okay, you're right. I am tired. But maybe in the morning?" she asked hopefully.

Warm lips nudged her neck and ear. "I'd be happy to oblige now, but in theory, you should be too tired to do anything but sleep."

With a little wiggle to a better position, she shifted closer to the growing ridge at her hips. When he shifted, lifted her thigh and slipped inside, she gasped and arched.

"Oh, dear God," she whispered.

"Okay?"

"Better than," she cried out on a whimper.

With his hands on her hips, he moved slowly in and out,

not doing anything more than enjoying the moment, and the sensation of being one with each other.

The climax when it came, took her by surprise.

Big waves of peace. Not ripping through her. Not exploding inside. Instead a gentle wash of sensation that rolled over and through her with joy.

Tremors still surged through her when she closed her eyes and dropped off to sleep.

Something about him was so damn caring.

"I could love him," she whispered to herself. "I really could."

And she smiled as she drifted off.

COULD SHE? THAT was something he wanted but hadn't exactly expected. This had all happened fast. Too fast. Maybe. And maybe not.

She was special. He had never denied that. But he hadn't expected to feel what he was. Or to experience the depths of her emotions either. But no doubt, this would be a connection he'd miss.

He held her close against him and let sleep take him too.

He had no idea what was going on in this world, but he needed to be fresh and ready for anything.

When the alarm ripped through the compound several hours later, he bolted awake and stood, ready for whatever danger was present. Turning, he was quick to get his prosthesis on and then dressed. By the time he looked at the bed, Lissa was sitting up with the bedcovers clutched to her chest, staring at him in shock.

"What was that?" she asked.

"An intruder alert. Stay here. I'll be back as soon as I can."

"Oh, hell, no." She bounced out the other side of the

bed and jumped into her clothes.

A sight he would've enjoyed any other time but not now as he was exposed.

She turned to look at him as she watched him pull his pants up over his prosthetic leg.

Hardly any light filtered into the room, but enough was here that he knew she'd see some of it. But what she said afterward surprised him.

"The next time we go to bed, I want to explore your body. It seems like you're always taking care of me. But you're so big and beautiful, I really want to appreciate yours too."

And damn if he didn't feel an erection coming on. Just the thought was so damn enticing. He brushed it all aside and said, "Next time."

And now he'd do his damnedest to make sure that there was one because that thought would keep him on the edge, and full of anticipation, until it happened.

But first they had a problem on the compound.

He slipped over to the door and held out his hand. "You're to stay with me. No going off in any other direction. I need to know exactly where you are at all times." In his other hand he held his handgun.

She looked at it and swallowed. "It's likely to be them, isn't it?"

"I sure as hell hope it is. I'm more than ready to beat these assholes to the ground."

"Me too. Lead the way," she said with a smile.

He opened the door and peered around the edge of the doorframe into the darkened hallway. With his hand firmly grasping hers, he led her to the stairs.

For better or worse, he'd rather have her at his side than anywhere else.

Now to find out what the problem was.

Chapter 17

W ITH HER HEART pounding, she followed Stone into the dark hallway. She had no idea what time it was, but moonlight came in the window at the end of the hallway so she'd estimate two in the morning. She called that the witching hour. That's when every asshole came out to do their dirty work. And for all the nerves rippling through her chest, closing in tight against her, she felt fine because she was with Stone.

With the grip of his fingers on her hand, she knew he had no intention of letting her go. And that meant she was exactly where she wanted to be. Of course the circumstances could be different, but she was damn glad she wasn't alone.

Downstairs on the main floor Levi stood in the center of the lobby, searching in all four directions as if looking for something to indicate where the trouble was. Just as suddenly as it had started, the loud clashing alarm stopped.

Silence reigned. Normally she'd be delighted, but right now, she just took that as another bad sign. She felt Stone's hand tighten on hers.

He gave her a quick reassuring smile, brought her hand up to his lips, and dropped a kiss along her knuckles. Instantly her stress eased.

If he wasn't worried, then she would let him handle this. Apparently it was what he did. She trusted him. So far he hadn't let her down. Neither did she want anything to happen to him. He was a hell of a good man.

He led her toward the kitchen, and they stopped just short of the doorway. He peered around the corner and then took her inside. In a low whisper, he said, "Rhodes, what's up?"

When Rhodes turned around, she gasped. She hadn't seen the silent figure against the wall between the two windows. She couldn't get any closer to Stone, but she tried. In the dark, Rhodes looked to be one big scary-ass dude. And she realized she was snuggling up to Stone, who was one of the baddest-looking dudes she'd ever met.

Rhodes's low whisper finally penetrated her mind. "No sign of an intruder in the house, nor did I see anyone in the yard. But something tripped the alarm."

Stone nodded. "Haven't had it tripped accidentally by animals since we fixed the height."

"Doesn't mean it couldn't be something bigger though."

"Who's in the control room?"

"Ice, and Levi's heading there."

"I'll take Lissa up and leave her with them and come back down. We can do a full sweep together."

"Make it fast," Rhodes said. "Don't like sitting here. I'll check to make sure we don't have any of our weaknesses compromised."

Lissa was still trying to figure out what that last part actually meant when Stone led her to the hall and then the stairway. He never said a word as he took her to the top floor. She hadn't been up here yet. He brought her down to a simple door that could've been a bedroom or closet for how innocuous it looked. He knocked once, then twice, then again. Without making a sound, it opened under his hand.

Ice stood there. She glanced from Stone to Lissa. Then she opened the door wider. "Come in, Lissa. Grab a chair over by the corner if you like."

She turned toward Stone as Lissa made her way inside the small room full of computers and monitors—as in one hell of a security system. In the background she heard Ice say to Stone, "Looks like somebody tried to climb the fence at the top of the ridge."

"I'll go check it out," Stone said. "Just keep watch. Let's make sure that wasn't a decoy."

"So far there's no sign of anything else outside," Levi said. "Merk went down to check out the two entrances."

"Send Harrison with him then," Ice said. "Everybody needs to be in twos right now."

Stone frowned. "We're a little short on men for that."

Ice turned a pained gaze on him. Lissa was surprised he didn't melt. Ice might be less than half Stone's weight, but something was just so damn commanding about her.

Their voices dropped into a hushed whisper, then Stone left. The door closed as silently as it had opened, and Ice returned to her chair in front of the monitors.

There wasn't a whole lot for Lissa to do or say, so she stayed quiet and watched. She'd never seen a system like this. Not only was it massive, but it appeared to be cutting edge. On the monitors she could see various sites outside—the buildings in the compound—as well as rooms inside the house.

She had no idea where Stone was actually going. She studied the monitors, hoping to catch sight of him.

Then she gasped and leaned forward. A man dressed in black with a weapon of some sort, appeared to be on the ground by the fence. In a low voice she asked, "Is that

Stone?"

"No," Levi's voice was curt. He picked up a headset, put it on his head, and said, "Stone, can you hear me?"

She watched anxiously as the man on the ground lined up a rifle. Shit. Pointing at somebody or at the house itself. Either way was bad news. Stone was going out there, and he was unprepared. She clenched her hands into fists as Levi continued trying to raise Stone.

Levi switched to calling someone else.

There was only silence.

"Logan, we've got a sniper on the top fourth corner. He's taking aim. Stone went out alone."

Then Levi's hands fell to work on the keyboard. Apparently whoever was on the other end of the communication line had answered. She could hardly sit in the chair. To know Stone was walking into an ambush was more than she could stand. She jumped up and walked to the window, like that would help, as if she could see something and yell at him.

Instantly Ice snapped, "Sit down."

She turned back, not quite understanding, and then realized if she was in the window, she was a target too. Quickly she moved behind the stone wall and slowly sank to the floor. And then the shakes came.

She wrapped her arms around her knees and tucked them up close to her chest.

"Just stay where you are. You'll be fine," Levi said.

"Or you can go back to the chair. Just don't stand in the window where your reflection will show. Enough targets to keep track of right now. We don't need you getting hit by a sniper," Ice said.

Lissa raised her gaze to stare at Ice, who was doing a

damn good job of modeling her name. "How can you guys be so calm?" she cried in a low voice. "When you talk about snipers, shooting, and killing people, you don't even blink," she finished weakly.

"We're used to it. This is what we do." Ice's focus never left the monitors in front of her.

Lissa watched Ice as she clicked on a few keys, and something shifted on the screen, but Lissa hadn't really realized what had been there so didn't understand what was there now. It was confusing, but at the same time, almost awe-inspiring.

"We'll look after you," Levi said. "You'll be fine."

"I'll be fine?" she cried out. "I don't give a damn about me. What about Stone? He went out into an ambush."

Both Ice and Levi turned to look at her. And maybe it was her imagination, but she thought she saw approval in both their expressions.

Maybe it was just what she had wanted to see. She lifted her head, her gaze to the monitor, and gasped. She pointed. "I just saw a flash."

And realized that the sniper had fired. Most likely on Stone.

STONE REALIZED ALMOST instantly that his comm unit was out. Although a problem, not a major one. He could hear the tapping of Morse code on his headset. And that was good enough for him. He listened to the series of dots and dashes. A sniper was on the hill.

Stone changed directions and came around the back, creeping up the hill on the far side so he could see where the sniper hid. Stone lay down flat on the ground and studied the layout. They'd all done extensive night training here to make sure they knew every inch of this section. As Harrison said, the weaknesses were the ones that got you. And Stone had no intention of letting an asshole like this get into their place.

The sniper made no sense. He was taking a hell of a chance. Probably not a professional as much as a hired gun. For some, the distinction was nonexistent, but for Stone, it was major. Professionals were soldiers with lots of arms and military tactical training. A hired gun was somebody who would pick up a gun and shoot. Often they were damn good too.

But they didn't have the same background or discipline as the mercenaries. Stone heard a *ping*. Flattened on the ground as he was, it came nowhere near him, but gave him enough data to see where the shooter was. Stone picked up his night goggles and checked out the sniper, realizing Levi had been right. Black jeans, black T-shirt, and what looked like a hunting rifle. Not a professional, mercenary, or terrorist. They'd have better weapons.

So who the hell was this and why? Stone studied the layout and the man's exit avenues. With any luck, Harrison could set up on the one, and Stone the other. Between them, they'd pull this guy off his perch and bring him in. To that end, Stone shifted down the hill as quietly as possible.

There had been no rain in a long time; the ground was dusty. Both good and bad. It made for a smoother walk but left a trail. He went from peak to peak, saw a little bit of wild grass, and made his way over to it. He tested his comm system again and found it now worked. He sent a message to Harrison, telling him where everything was happening. They could use a few more men just in case. He didn't know how fast this shooter could run. It would be easy enough to end up in a long-distance pursuit. Something Stone didn't want.

Not when weapons were involved.

The sniper would have a vehicle somewhere close. It needed to be found and guarded. If the other men on his team used the hidden passageway, that would take them out around the corner of the road and effectively pin anybody between them. It would extend to the far ridges too.

A passageway they needed to complete fast. This was the second time the compound had come under siege in as many months. Sure they'd had half a dozen other jobs in the meantime, but this wasn't cool.

The compound was meant to be home. To be safe and secure. There'd been talk about some of the men moving out, living in the closest town, and that was always an option. Levi was also talking about bringing in contract men that they all trusted but who would live in various parts of the country. That was also good. But nothing quite like the tightness of the unit who lived or fought together.

From his new vantage point, Stone lifted his weapon, lined up a shot, and slammed a bullet into the fence post in front of the man's head.

His cry echoed across the valley. Realizing he'd been found out, the man ran straight downhill. He made no attempt to hide his tracks. This was a flat-out race for freedom. Only Stone was already halfway down the hill himself.

"Stone, I see him," Logan snapped in his earpiece. "I'm on the road. I should be able to cut him off."

"You do that. I'll meet you at the far side on the compound. Let's make sure this asshole doesn't get away." Harrison's voice disappeared as quickly as it came.

Stone grinned. This shooter had no idea what he was up against. They were effectively boxing him in. Pretty damn soon they'd have him. As Stone watched, he saw the headlights shine over the compound as Logan drove out of the gates. He quickly made his way across the low ridge, so he could see down the other side. Sure enough an old beat-up truck sat below, Logan driving toward it. The sniper was farther out than Logan; but Harrison would grab the intruder soon. So which direction would the man take? Stone hoped the sniper would break toward Stone. He wanted to get his hands on him.

Knowing Levi was watching the situation, Stone considered the possibilities. "Levi, I need you to be ready." And he quickly explained the options for the sniper.

"Got it," Levi said calmly. "Rhodes and Merk are searching outside the compound. Rhodes is in front of the compound, Merk the opposite side."

Perfect. Stone squatted down and watched. He'd have to make a decision as soon as the man came around the bend. And sure enough, the sniper caught sight of Logan pulling up behind his truck. He hit the brakes and came to a complete stop.

Which way would the shooter go?

Stone grinned with anticipation. *Let him come to me, please.* The sniper broke to the right—in line with Stone's path.

Chapter 18

WHEN THE ACTION started, Lissa bolted to the chair beside Levi. "Oh, my God! He got him," Lissa cheered.

"Of course he did," Ice said complacently. "Stone's big, but he moves like a panther. And he is very good at strategy."

"I believe you," Lissa said. "I've never seen the warrior in him quite like this. Sure, in Afghanistan, he was there and played a huge part in getting us out, but I think Merk and Rhodes were actually in the room and blew the window bars off." She sat back, relief washing through her. "It is something to see Stone in action."

"He's a good man." Levi stood up, took off his headset, patted Ice on the shoulder, and turned, walking out of the room, closing the door quietly behind him.

As Lissa watched on the monitor, she could see Stone shepherding his prisoner to the truck where Logan was. It took a few minutes, but then both vehicles were driven into the compound, convoy style. She realized that's where Levi had gone. To handle business down in the yard.

"I wondered if Stone's leg would've affected him," she admitted. "We haven't really talked about his disability, but, from watching him on that hillside, I'd never have known."

Ice laughed. "He's very determined not to let it make a difference in his life. When it first happened, we were all stunned, and then immediately we remembered this was Stone. That man can handle anything," she admitted. "Only that wasn't fair, because he still had to adjust. It didn't matter how capable, good, or awesome he was, he still lost a major part of his body, and it will take time to deal with the fallout."

"More time than anyone really realizes, I think," Lissa said. "The stump is a bit puffy-looking. And sometimes he hisses when he puts on the prosthesis."

Ice turned to study Lissa's face. "He gets sidelined if he does too much. He's actually been forced into office duty because he stayed on it longer than he should," she said with a smile. "I know he still pushes it, but it's way better than it used to be."

"He needs a better design for the leg." Lissa studied Ice. "Does he have a physiotherapist or specialist who works with him?"

"Of course. Plus, many doctors and engineers. The problem is taking his leg to a whole new level." At that Ice laughed. "And that means a lot more going on in that replacement leg than normal."

"A whole new level?" Lissa wasn't sure if she should ask.

She'd seen the man in action. She almost couldn't imagine. But then she thought about how alert he always was, how aware and protective. And that he carried a weapon with confidence, almost like it was a part of him. And what a liability not having that leg could be, but he'd turned it into the opposite.

"Oh, I know." She grinned. "He's trying to figure out how to turn it into a weapon."

Ice stood up and laughed. "I see you're getting to know him."

"In many ways, yes, but not anywhere near enough," Lissa admitted.

Ice walked to the door. Before she opened it, she turned and said, "Make sure if you walk down that path, you're prepared to go the distance." She studied Lissa's face for a long moment. "He was betrayed before. A mistake that cost him his leg. The guy is due for some good times, not more hard ones."

Ice turned and opened the door for someone, somehow knowing he stood on the other side.

Alfred walked in with a tray in his hands. "Coffee and a treat, ladies."

Lissa jumped to her feet and ran over. "Oh, my goodness, how did you know?"

"How did I know you would be starving? Because I noticed how much you eat at any one time." He grinned. "Ice is the same way. So I brought double portions for both of you." He walked over and set the tray down on the small table. "Looks like it'll be a very early morning here. The prisoner has just been brought into the compound. You're staying here?"

"Yes." Lissa glanced at Ice and then at Alfred. "I'll stay here until Stone's free."

"I'll tell him." Alfred walked out the door, closing it quietly behind him.

Lissa suddenly wondered at his question. "Does that make me a prisoner?" she asked slowly.

Ice turned to stare at her. "No," Ice said calmly. "It means you're always to be with someone. Never alone."

"Oh," Lissa said in a small voice. "Because I can't be trusted?" She'd really rather know how the land lay on that topic. If she wasn't welcome, she didn't want to be here.

But Ice's response surprised her. She laughed freely, the light sound tinkling around the room. "Good Lord, no. If we didn't trust you, you wouldn't be within one hundred miles of here. It's because you're a target and we have to make sure we keep you safe."

"Oh. Okay, that's much better." She reached for a huge muffin and took a bite.

Ice stared at her. "You know, very few people would think that being a target was much better than not being trusted."

"Maybe it's because they don't have my father. He never trusted me to do anything, nor my word," she mumbled around her bite. "Gives one a complex, you know?"

"I'm sure it does. But it's well past time to leave behind your father and whatever influence he had over you and begin a new life. You've been your own person for a long time. Don't stop now."

Lissa stared at the very intuitive woman. "You're right, you know?"

Ice nodded. "Yep, I am." She picked up one of the other muffins on the plate and said, "We see it all the time in the military. As a child, you join a family unit. Then grow and mature, gaining confidence and separating. In your case, you needed to leave to achieve that. Maybe you did that years ago. I don't know, but, with all this chaos going on, knowing that someone is trying to hurt you, it does make you want to revert back to being a little girl, looking for your parents to take care of you. However ..."

"However, as they barely ever took care of me before, my fallback plan isn't working." Lissa studied the muffin in her hand, but her thoughts were on her past as she thought about Ice's words because that was exactly what had happened. "I just don't want to have transference issues from my father to Stone," she admitted quietly. "I really like Stone, but I don't want to put that burden on anybody. And in my next relationship, I want a partner, not a father figure."

"Damn good thing," Ice said cheerfully. "Stone is nobody's idea of a father figure. He's a hell of a good man. But he also needs a partner. He doesn't need somebody that he's forced to look after. A limpet attached to his side for him to be the big bad hero. That man lives that same scenario. He needs somebody who can walk beside him and hold him when he needs it, help him make decisions when they have to be made. Not just someone looking at him to create the world she wants to live in. Relationships are all about both people making their lives work together."

How very perceptive of the woman. It said a lot about her relationship with Levi. They looked great together physically, and yet that affection and caring obviously went deep between them.

"You're right. But Stone is a big presence to live up to. I'm not sure I'm good enough," she admitted quietly. "That's been a problem for me since forever. Men who are bigger than life and expect more than I can give. Men who give decrees, and expect people to follow them, and do it so perfectly they're never disappointed."

"Stone's not like that. He's not like your father in any way. And that's something you need to separate out very clearly. They always say women marry their fathers. But I also happen to think we marry the qualities we like in our fathers and we're happy to ditch the parts we don't want. If your father was an alcoholic, it doesn't mean you have to marry one. But, if your father was a very generous, caring animal lover, maybe that's the part of him you want to take forward into your next relationship. It's all about balance. And when things go off balance, it gets very hellish."

"And you're speaking from experience, I presume."

"I am. Thankfully most of that's in the past. Relationships aren't too much work when you're with the right person, but they are something that you work at."

"Oh, I like that phrase. No one ever explained it in that way." Lissa reached for a second muffin. She ate half of it in silence as she thought about Ice's words. "Does everybody live here in the compound?"

Ice shot her a look and then nodded. "Lately everybody does. Several apartments are being outfitted and some of the men will move into those instead of the rooms. But like everything else, it's a work in progress."

There was silence for a few moments as Ice's gaze moved constantly from the monitors to Lissa and back. "What's worrying you?"

"My relationship with Stone actually." Lissa shrugged. "You know, there's the normal dating thing, and then the nights over at various places, followed by the living together." She laughed. "We sort of skipped all the other parts and just jumped into the last. I'm afraid I've intruded in some way."

"So maybe rather than worry, you should talk to Stone about taking some time out just for the two of you to go to a movie or for a meal, even take a picnic out in the blue yonder and just discuss things."

Lissa brightened at that idea. "Actually that sounds lovely." Her mind was spinning. Possibilities wafted in and out. Because that was exactly what she needed—time with Stone.

Then Ice burst her bubble. "You'll have to wait until this problem is solved," Ice reminded her. "No taking off just the two of you when we have snipers following us to the house."

"Right." Reality crashed in once again.

HE DIDN'T KNOW if it was by accident or deliberate that he could overhear parts of the conversation through Ice's headset, but thankfully his comm unit worked just fine now. Either way Stone was damn grateful for the opportunity to hear the girls talk. It surprised him, but it also made him feel a whole lot better about Lissa. And Ice was right; he and Lissa needed time together to talk. But reality was a bitch, and right now Levi was questioning a sniper sitting in a chair inside the compound.

"Is there any point asking more questions when the ass-hole isn't answering?" Stone asked Levi. "Why not call the authorities? They're just a phone call away."

Merk and Rhodes remained silent but gave a small nod Levi's way.

Harrison snorted. "Screw that. Without answers, we'll just dig a ditch out back and dump him in. Remember that comment about a mass grave? We really need to work on that."

From the looks of the man sitting in the chair he was of Mexican descent, likely a rebel from across the border needing the money and so he took on the job. He'd talk if they forced it out of him, but they probably couldn't trust what came from his mouth.

Suddenly Stone was sick of the whole mess. He looked at Levi and said, "Just kill the asshole. None of it matters anyway."

Levi turned, walked to the bench, and picked up a handgun. He checked that it was loaded and turned around to face the man in the chair.

Something about Stone's voice or Levi's actions said they meant business and really didn't give a shit if the shooter lived or died because all of a sudden, the man took notice.

"No, wait."

Levi stopped and looked at him. But a bored look was on his face, as if to say, *Make it good or else.* "I'm listening. Better be something worthwhile. I've already lost enough sleep this night."

"I got a phone call. The person asked me to check out the property."

"Who called you, when, and why?" Levi crossed his arms over his chest and leaned back against the workbench.

"I don't know the man's name. We don't ask questions like that. He said there'd be cash for the information, if it was any good." The man spread his hands. "Cash is a little thin on the ground these days. I needed the money."

"What information were you supposed to give him?"

"He wanted to know how many people were here and the kind of setup you had. He understood this was a large property, and I needed to drive partway and walk the rest. But I couldn't get any closer without being seen."

The man's face oozed earnestness. Stone tended to believe him.

"How were you to get the information to him, and where was your money to be sent?" Levi asked.

Stone walked from one side to the other, his mind busy. No renovations had been done lately, though they were gearing up to do two more apartments. But they hadn't had any workmen in recently. They didn't even get mail delivered here. Everything was picked up in town. On purpose. Everybody who came through the gates to this place had to be vetted and security here had to be tight. They'd been busy with jobs of their own.

The odd person drove down the road, saw the locked gates, turned, and left again. And there had been a couple of those.

They could check the camera feed to get the vehicles' license plates. That was a hell of a damn good idea.

Isolation wasn't everything, but it sure removed a lot of variables in a situation like this.

To Levi, Stone said, "I'll go check out the surveillance cameras. See if we've had any 'lost' vehicles around lately. Might have been the man who called him."

"Good idea. In the meantime, I'll get the rest of the information out of this asshole."

Chapter 19

W HEN THE KNOCK sounded on the door, Lissa already knew who stood there. She could see his face from the hallway monitors. That was how Ice had seen Alfred arrive earlier. Lissa looked at Ice and asked, "Can I open it?"

Ice nodded, her gaze never leaving the monitors in front of her. Lissa opened the door and smiled up at Stone. She stepped back so he could enter.

He came in, his voice low when he asked, "How are you doing?"

She beamed. "I'm fine, thanks. How are you? You're the one who went out there after that man."

He let that roll off his shoulders with a shrug and proceeded to pull up a chair beside Ice. "Ice, do you have the video feed for the last few days? Maybe go back as far as a week. We're looking for any vehicles that came to the compound and turned around, as if expecting something else to be here. You know, like if the person was lost. We want the license plates and if we can, pictures of the driver. Somehow someone knew we were here. And if they followed us in, they would have known it was one way."

"Unless they use Google Earth," Lissa said, listening to the conversation with interest. "I do that all the time. It would've shown the road stops and that a big compound was here."

Ice turned the monitor setup to run the feed, then hit Start. Lissa and Stone sat side by side and watched as it ran in Fast Forward. They slowed the video as a car drove up six days ago with an older couple in it. They got out and stared, then shrugged, turned the car around, and headed into town.

"I presume they were just lost?" Lissa said.

"Probably."

It also made sense if it was an older couple. She turned her head to watch the feed moving again.

Two days ago a truck came in, pulled up at the curve before the gate, and parked. For ten minutes the driver sat and surveyed the compound. Stone leaned in, then quickly adjusted the monitor to get a close-up. He froze. "That's him," he snapped. "That's the guy we're holding downstairs."

"I thought you said you were looking for somebody different?"

"That's what he said."

"Is it possible somebody else came by earlier than a week ago?" Lissa asked.

"Sure, we get people all the time," Ice said. "But if this relates to you, then it happened since we rescued you from Afghanistan."

"Oh." She had forgotten about that. "So maybe we should run the last day and a half and see if there was a second vehicle?"

Stone hit the button, and the feed continued. On the other side of them, having marked down the date and time stamp, Ice brought up a different feed from the ridge. Lissa's gaze went from one side to the other, trying to take it all in. As soon as they ran through the rest of the time and realized no other vehicles had showed up on the one monitor, they shifted to the other she had set up and hit Play. Sure enough a truck turned around without coming into the compound and headed back the way it came. They could only watch his tracks for a few miles before the feed lost sight of it.

Stone stood up to study the man's face clearly on the feed.

"Could you positively identify the driver from that monitor image? I can barely make out his features." Lissa asked. "Or is it possible it just looks like him?" With the two of them staring at her, Lissa shrugged. "I'm just wondering if you mistook the identity of the driver, and there are actually two people."

"I suspect it's the same driver both times," Stone said. "And he's trying to throw us offtrack by making it seem like there's somebody else. I do think he was probably contacted and hired for this job, yet that person did not come here himself." Stone walked to the doorway. "He wouldn't take that step if he were trying to stay hidden."

That made a strange kind of sense to her too. She hopped up to her feet impulsively and said, "Can I come with you?"

He turned to her, looked over at Ice, and then nodded. "We got the culprit downstairs," he said. He held out his hand. "You might as well come and see if you recognize him."

"No reason why I would," she said as she left the room.

Stone closed the door securely behind them, leaving Ice locked in again.

"Is there always somebody in that room?" Lissa asked.

"No, but when we're having security issues, like we are right now, then somebody is always tracking."

She nodded. "That actually makes me feel a lot better."

"It doesn't necessarily take people to keep the entire system running," he said quietly. "It runs automatically twenty-four hours a day. But it doesn't send out alerts if somebody is seen, so we need to be watching the monitors to see an intruder in real time. However, the feeds are always there to refer back to every day, and you can bet we do check."

"I hadn't considered that your job might be this dangerous," she said. "I figured this was all just because of me."

He laughed. "It might be right now," he said, "but this place was attacked a month ago, and that had nothing to do with you."

"So you're in danger living here?"

As he was several steps ahead of her, he stopped, turned to look at her, and said, "No, absolutely not. This is probably the safest place any of us could be right now."

She nodded, but it was hard to equate. "My life used to be very calm and quiet," she said. "Never any of this danger or secrecy."

"Most of the time we don't have any either. But it's our job in the private security business to handle trouble all over the world and we try to make sure we don't bring those problems home." He stepped in front of her, still standing on the stairs, and said, "Don't forget. We were all well-trained in the military and we're good at what we do. There'll always be assholes out there. And there'll always be a need for people like us to stand up for the little people."

She smiled. "You really are heroes, aren't you?"

He laughed. "Yes, *heroes for hire*."

"Oh, my gosh, that's a great name."

He turned to look at her, his eyebrows raised, and said, "Hell, no. We don't see ourselves as heroes. We're just men."

"Men with a very particular skill set," she argued. "If you

were to advertise, oh my, you would make a killing."

His voice still teasing but with a cooler tone, he said, "Not happening."

She'd been so engrossed in the conversation that she didn't notice where he was taking her. She stopped in the doorway to see the rest of the men gathered around somebody seated on a chair. And she realized this was the man who'd shot at Stone.

Suddenly rage washed over her. She walked right up to him, hefted her arm back, and smacked him hard across the face. She could hear the gasps from the other men and heard Stone say, "Whoa, easy there."

But instead of listening, she shoved her face into the stranger's and said, "And that's for trying to shoot one of the guys." Then she stepped back to stand beside Stone, linking her arm with his. Under her breath she muttered, "Asshole."

The other men took one look at the intruder in the chair, back to her, then to the shooter again—and they grinned.

NOW SHE'D DONE it. Stone wanted to roll his eyes, but inside he was grinning too. It took a lot of gumption to stand up to somebody like that, and to think she'd done it in his defense was just great.

But he also knew the guys would never let him live this down. He glared at them, his gaze flicking from Rhodes's big smirk to Merk's grin to Levi's cold and hard face though his eyes twinkled. Nobody had missed it. Even Logan and Harrison were coughing and holding their hands to their mouths.

The intruder just stared at her in shock. "I didn't shoot

at nobody, bitch."

She gasped and stepped forward, her hand swinging behind her again. Stone quickly grabbed her and pulled her to his side. "It's okay, honey. We'll deal with him."

"But he's lying," she said in outrage. "I saw him shoot at you. Asshole."

This time the man just shut up and glared at her.

Stone instinctively stepped in front of her, blocking her from the man's rage. "We already know what you did. I wanted to see if she could identify you, see if any shared history had brought you into her life."

"I don't give a shit about the bitch." The man spat in the ground. "A bullet would be the best answer for her." This time Stone's fist came out and slammed into the man's jaw.

Instead of snapping back as he'd done from Lissa's slap, the man's head lolled to the side. Stone had knocked him unconscious.

"Stone, we weren't quite done talking to him," Levi said in exasperation.

Splash.

Everybody swore and stepped back as a bucket of ice-cold water rained over the intruder's face. They turned to glare at Lissa, standing, holding the empty bucket in her hand. She said, "Now Stone can go at him again."

And sure enough the intruder shook his head as he came back to consciousness. The men just looked at Stone, back to her, then shook their heads.

"Wow, you got a live one this time," Merk told Stone.

"This time?" She jutted her jaw out at Merk, who immediately wiped the smile off his face. "I'm the last one," she snapped. She turned back toward Stone, who was studying her as if he didn't know what to make of her. She grinned.

"You might have a history, honey, but I'm your future. Get used to it." She reached up and placed a kiss on his chin, which was as high up as she could reach, then turned to glare at the others and snapped, "And don't any of you be forgetting that."

She turned and stormed out.

Stone watched her go. He couldn't believe what she'd done or said. But at the same time, both had made him smile. Then he laughed. Great big belly ones that rolled through the massive garage. When he finally calmed down, the others still stood in the circle, around the intruder, but stared at Stone. He grinned, his chuckles still escaping, and said, "Don't look at me for answers. I don't have any. She's something I've never seen before."

"You can say that again," Levi said. "You sure you're up for that?"

But Stone couldn't take the grin off his face, nor did he want to squelch the joy running through his system. It seemed like he had lived such a serious and dark life for so long that she was a breath of fresh air. With Lissa being unpredictable and definitely unique, maybe he wasn't quite sure he was up for it, but he'd be damned if he would walk away from the opportunity.

"I better be," he said with a smile. "Otherwise she'll eat me alive."

At that the whole group burst into laughter.

Chapter 20

LISSA DIDN'T KNOW why the hell she'd shared her expectations. It was stupid as hell. She and Stone were too far away from anything like a relationship-status declaration. What the hell did she do? It just made no sense.

She blamed the asshole in the chair. She'd seen red when she realized he'd been the one who had shot at Stone. And when he blacked out, she just wanted to hit him again. So she tossed the water on him. But all she'd really done was give the rest of the guys a laugh.

She lifted a shaky hand to her brow and wished she had some self-control. She really was a stupid, impulsive fool. Her father was right. He kept telling her, *You have to stop and think about the repercussions of your actions.* It seemed like that was all she'd ever heard growing up. Apparently it hadn't done any good because here she was, still being foolish.

She walked into the kitchen and sat down at the table where she could just be alone for a moment—only to realize she wasn't. A cup of coffee was placed in front of her. She turned to look at Alfred. "Thank you," she said sadly. "I really don't belong here, do I?"

His eyebrows shot up, and he walked around the table, pulled the chair out across from her, and sat down. "Why would you say that?"

"If you'd seen what I just did …" She shook her head. "I'm a fool."

"And sometimes we all need that breath of fresh air," Alfred said. "Just because you're different doesn't mean you don't fit in."

She looked at him blankly.

"These guys have way-too-much military training, discipline, and regimentation in their world. They need laughter, light, and some sunshine. It's very important."

She looked at him and wondered if he was just trying to make her feel better. "It's been way too fast and easy. Well, okay, maybe not that last one, but definitely been the first."

"What, you and Stone?"

She nodded. "He probably thinks I'm an idiot."

"Stone's always had to be strong and tough," Alfred said quietly. "It's expected of him. To think that you are somebody he's attracted to, that just makes my heart warm and gives me hope for his future."

She looked at him curiously. "Why?"

"Because it means it's something that he really wants in his life. He wants happiness, laughter. The four men that started all this—Rhodes, Merk, Levi, and Stone—they did some of the ugliest, deepest, darkest, nastiest jobs the military could throw at them. They always came through with flying colors, except for the last mission," he said. "It changes a person to see and do all that. Stone doesn't have to live on that level of darkness anymore, but it'll take somebody like you to pull him into the light."

She drummed her fingers on her cheek as she studied Alfred's face. "Stone seems so strong and independent. So capable of being alone. It makes me feel like there isn't any room for me."

This time Alfred's smile, when it came, was slow and gentle. "It's not that there's no place for you. But he's been locked in tight to keep the world out. Hard to do but they all had to, and it'll take somebody very special to make a place for herself inside their circle."

"How does Ice fit into this?"

"She was the helicopter pilot who rescued them on their last SEAL mission," Alfred admitted. "Levi and Ice have finally got their issues worked out."

"I can't imagine Ice ever not having a place in that circle. They respect and like her."

"But that's also because she knows that's where she belongs. Imagine if one of them tried to tell her that she didn't."

Lissa grinned. "There'd be fireworks."

"Exactly." Alfred stood up from the chair and said, "Think about that." He picked up his coffee and walked away.

She stared after him, wondering if he was right. But in order for her to have that self-confidence, to feel she was exactly where she belonged, she had to know they could do nothing to move her out. She had to acknowledge that on an inside level.

But that meant she also had to connect with Stone a whole lot more. Although he had let her in, sometimes ... she didn't know if that was something he regretted. They hadn't had a chance to find out, all because this asshole had come into their lives.

So effectively the shooter was stopping her from having a future with Stone, and that just made her angry all over again.

And yet it wasn't just him. It was this whole mess. She

got up with her cup of coffee and sauntered to the room where the men were talking with the intruder. She didn't let him see her, in case the flow of words stopped when he caught sight of her. He obviously didn't like women, especially her.

And maybe she should start there.

When a lull in conversation came, she stepped around Stone, her hand automatically reaching up to clamp onto his elbow. She asked the intruder, "Why don't you like me?"

The intruder's face shut down, and he spat in her direction.

She felt Stone go rigid under her hand. She patted his big forearm and said gently, "It's okay. He obviously doesn't know me."

The intruder snapped, "And I wouldn't want to. You're nothing but a rich trust-fund bitch."

"Interesting." She studied the other men, realized they agreed. So this guy actually knew her, or about her.

"Is that the fuel your employer used to make you do this? Learning to hate somebody who has more money and was born with a silver spoon in her mouth? Someone useless, who doesn't understand the struggle, how you had to claw your way through life to get to where you are?"

He glared at her. "Exactly. People like you. Useless, can't do anything, born with money, die with money. You don't know what it's like for the rest of us."

She nodded. "Nothing I say will change your view of me. But it's interesting that that was the tool used to help you target me. I'm one of many so I would still like to know, why me?"

He snorted. "That's easy. Because even though you're a rich bitch, you figured you could cheat the system. But when you get into bed with the bad boys, you sure as hell better do the job or pay the price." He grinned. "In this case you didn't do the job but you took the money. So you're paying the price."

"Okay, I can see that would be your take on it. By the way, what exactly is the job I was supposed to do?"

"You were supposed to bring that shit into the country and hand it over. You were well-paid for the job. Now you'll pay for screwing them over."

"I wasn't paid for anything," she protested. She could sense the attention of all the men circling the two of them. But she also knew she didn't dare break eye contact because the shooter was finally talking.

"And what exactly was I supposed to bring over?" She kept her voice light and conversational. But it was hard because she was finally getting to the crux of the matter.

He snorted. "They didn't tell me exactly. But I understand it was some kind of experimental drug."

She turned to stare at Stone, then back at the intruder. "You do realize all my luggage was seized in the London airport, including that experimental drug, right?"

He frowned. "Heathrow?"

She nodded. "Yes, Heathrow. We flew back via London before we came here. All my luggage was taken, and I never had any of it to bring with me."

The intruder stared at her in shock, and then he laughed. "Oh, that's rich. Now there's nothing to save your sorry white hide." And he laughed some more. "Not while the drug companies are after you."

OVER BRUNCH THE topic was discussed at length. But the

one conclusion they'd all confirmed was that somebody had slipped the drugs into her bags, which were then seized at Heathrow. And whoever had slipped them in was expecting delivery here in the USA. With the drugs gone, and this person waiting for them, Lissa, as well as Levi's team, had a problem.

The intruder had given them only a little more, but had confirmed they were looking for medicine grade pharmaceuticals. With that information, Stone had a good idea what was going on, but needed proof. And he needed to get his hands on Kevin. There were more than a few questions he wanted to ask.

"It also means somebody from the refugee, or terrorist, camp, put the drugs into my bag," she said.

Stone stared down at her plate. She was hardly eating. It had been a pretty nerve-racking morning. He nudged her gently. "Eat up."

She nodded and lifted another bite to her mouth. She turned to Levi and asked, "Did you ever hear from Charles?"

"Just a couple messages. I have to call him back as soon as we're finished here." He smiled at her. "It's been a little busy this morning."

"Did you get an update on Kevin?"

He shook his head. "No, but I will be sure to ask Charles."

She nodded and kept quiet but wasn't eating again. She was toying with the food on her plate.

That worried Stone more than anything. He'd seen this girl eat. He polished off his plate and asked, "What's bothering you?"

"I'm worried that the same person who's behind all this may have killed Kevin ... and Susan."

Silence sat heavy in the room. Stone turned his gaze to the others. No wonder Lissa was worried. She'd worked with the two of them for months.

"I wasn't going to bring that up," she said quietly. "But I also have to consider they may have killed Marge."

"Are you thinking they saw or knew who might've put this into your luggage? Otherwise why kill them?"

"Or because the bad guys put it into their luggage too," she said. Tears filled her eyes. "There's just so much death right now, it seems like a logical link to wonder if maybe they weren't the first two deaths. Then Marge."

Levi nodded, quickly emptied his coffee cup, and stood up. "Time for me to check in with Charles." And he walked out.

Ice had already finished eating. She got up and walked off with him.

Lissa looked at Stone. "It's hard to think others were killed or hurt because of this."

"Whether they did or didn't, it is not your fault. The fact is that sometimes assholes move people around in this world like a chess game to take out good ones. It still doesn't mean you're responsible. But it does mean we have to do everything we can to make sure you are not next."

She wrapped her arms around her chest and nodded.

"And for that to happen, you have to eat." He nodded at her half-empty plate. "Finish this up, and I'll take you to get a nap again."

Her tone was dry but her words were teasing as she said, "There's the Stone I know. Always trying to get me into bed."

Stone glanced at the guys remaining in the room. Lissa had pretty much blown any cover their relationship had had with her speech earlier. He might as well be equally honest here. "I'm pretty sure it's the other way around." He laughed. "There's a lot worse things for me to do than that."

She quickly polished off her meal and stood up. He nodded to the rest of the crew and led her from the room. Upstairs on the second floor, he took her to his room and got her settled into bed. "Do you want me to stay here, or will you be okay?"

She smiled. "I'll be fine. There's a ton of people around this place."

"That there is. That doesn't mean they'll be watching out for you though. We can't always see when somebody's in trouble."

"Outside of this nightmare, I'll be fine." She curled deeper into the covers and closed her eyes.

He waited for a few minutes to make sure she actually drifted off. When he figured she was under, he walked to the door and took a last look. As a precaution he pulled out his keys and locked the door. At least she'd be locked in. She could get out if she wanted to, but it would be damn hard for anybody else to get in.

Then he headed to the office. Ice and Levi were both here. Levi was on a call to Charles.

Stone looked around and asked, "Whatever happened to Sienna?"

Ice never lifted her head from the paperwork in front of her. "She had a few things to settle up before moving here full time. She's expected next week."

"For real?" Stone was happy to hear that. She was a nice girl. She helped to improve the balance of the testosterone around the compound. It might also give Lissa a friend.

"Yes. Alfred drove her to the airport while we were in

Afghanistan."

"I must be really out of it, considering I didn't notice she was gone until now. That makes me feel like an idiot."

"Charles has news." Levi announced putting his phone down on the desk. "Kevin and Susan were almost destitute. Medical bills to the tune of hundreds of thousands of dollars, and their house in France has a second mortgage."

"Which is motive right there," Stone said.

"I've been trying to track his phone, but it's off or dead. Or he's ditched it," Ice said quietly. "There's something not right about him."

"Charles had another tidbit ..."

Stone turned to look at Levi. "What?"

"The initial tox report on Susan said an experimental drug was used on her, and not one they'd ever seen before."

"Interesting. It definitely fits." Stone thought about what such a drug could mean. "I wonder what the cause of death will end up being."

"Cardiac arrest at the moment," Levi said. "I spoke to Merk earlier, and he's found nothing on his pipeline. Neither has Rhodes so far."

"I'm not surprised," Ice said. "Once we get into the pharmaceutical market that opens the world up for suspects."

"Charles mentioned a company called Narque Ltd. It's well-known for being on the shady side of the law."

"Harold Jorgenson runs that outfit." Ice smiled at the look of surprise on their faces. "I've heard my father cuss about him and his company in the past. Jorgenson's reputation is pretty ugly."

"Right. So we need to send a message. Let them know Susan is dead and Kevin is missing. There is no drug or money." Stone nodded. "Easy, right?"

"Actually it might be." Ice turned to Levi. "Call Bullard."

Levi's eyebrows shot up. "Good idea." He was already making the call.

Stone walked over and sat on a spare chair. "I hardly know Sienna."

At that, Ice lifted her head and smirked. "I think you've got another girl on your brain, Stone. Sienna just didn't quite make the cut."

"She's a nice girl, but I think she's much more Rhodes's style."

Ice tilted her head to the side and looked at him. "Interesting. Why him?"

He shrugged. "There's a chemistry there."

Ice nodded. "You saw that, did you?"

"Oh, yeah, I saw it. I think everybody did."

"Just because there's chemistry doesn't mean it's right."

Stone stopped and studied her for a moment. "Is that directed at me or Rhodes?"

She raised that flat gaze of hers to him and added, "Whichever fits."

He studied her for a long moment. "Do you have a problem with Lissa?" He'd really rather know up front because if he did start a relationship—hell, he was well past the starting point, but if something was developing here, they all lived in close quarters.

She shook her head. "No, actually I really like her. She's got gumption. And that's worth a lot. But she's also a softy. And you have the power to break her heart."

He winced. "Did you ever consider that maybe she has the power to break mine?"

At that Ice smiled. And when she did, it was easy to see

the goddess within. In a soft, gentle voice she said, "That's how it's supposed to be."

Levi finished his call and turned to join them again. "Bullard knows Jorgenson. He'll make the call but can't promise anything."

"Good enough. We've done what we can for now. This might get him off our backs." Stone shrugged. "And it might not. If Kevin is still alive, he better have the goods, all their money, or one hell of a good hiding place to live the rest of his life."

Stone agreed with a short nod, then studied Levi a moment and said, "I know it's really early yet regarding my relationship with Lissa, but aren't a couple of the rooms being rehabbed into apartments?"

Levi nodded. "And one of them was slated for you, no doubt about that. I don't know what she does, or if she even needs to do anything jobwise, but that's something that'll have to be considered as well." He studied Stone. "Are you sure you're ready for this? You barely know her."

"I know. And maybe not, but let's be prepared just in case it does work out. Besides, she needs a place to stay in the meantime. After this is over, who knows?" Stone stared off in the distance. It *was* fast. But it was also something he didn't want to *not* be ready for. He nodded. "I don't know the truth about her financial situation either. But she'll have to make some decisions about that herself." He settled down in the chair between the two of them. "I actually find myself in a position I hadn't expected to be in."

"She's young, but not that much," Ice said quietly. "Remember, it's only girls who would be upset by the amputation. For a woman, it wouldn't even make her blink."

Maybe for the first time Stone believed that.

He thought back to most of the women he'd spent time with, not just over the last year but decade. They'd all been short-term relationships. More of a good time, not a long-term type of thing. Although they might consider it fun having sex with a one-legged man, he really didn't see any of them handling it for any length of time.

That didn't say much about his judgment where women were concerned. And yet ... this situation was very different. He was pretty sure Lissa had noticed his leg at the beginning. Yet, in bed, she didn't seem to care.

Chapter 21

W HEN LISSA WOKE up the next time, it was like a homecoming. She'd been in Stone's bed just long enough now that it felt right. She was also in no rush to leave. As matter of fact, she wished she could have what she'd called a pyjama day in which she didn't have to get dressed but could just laze around in bed the whole day. Seemed like a long time since her life had been calm enough to allow for something like that. Memories came flashing back about the sniper and all the security crap that had gone on here of late.

She shuffled around to sit up and lean back against the headboard. She reached for her new phone. She'd been asleep for hours according to the time.

She studied her phone and then decided to try a couple people she knew from the refugee camp. She pulled out the napkin she'd written all her contacts on and saw Kevin's name.

She really needed to put them into her phone. She quickly dialed his number. It was a long shot. Half of the people involved in this nightmare expected Kevin to be dead. But she always had hope. Maybe it had just gotten to be too much, and he had walked away.

Hell, she could see that happening at any time.

If she'd just lost her husband, was stuck in a foreign country, and didn't have a way to handle any of the logistics involved in dealing with the police investigation, or burying her spouse, she could see being so stressed she might just walk away. And they could all be looking for a boogeyman.

The phone rang and rang and just as she went to shut it off, a man picked up and said, "Hello?"

She grinned. "Kevin?"

"Yes, who's this?"

She bounced in her bed, shuffling higher against the headboard. "It's Lissa," she cried. "Oh, my God! I finally reached you."

But an odd silence fell on the other end of the phone. And then the man said in a hard tone, "I'm sorry. Wrong number. Don't call here again."

And he hung up.

She stared in shock. "I could swear that was his voice. And he said yes to his name," she said out loud to herself. She stared down at the phone but didn't know what to do. And then she realized she had to tell someone. She slipped out of bed, phone in hand, and headed up to the control room. She didn't know if Stone would be there, but she was sure somebody would be at the monitors.

She hoped so. She gave a quick rap on the door. She didn't remember the specific number Stone had used earlier, but if they were watching the monitors, somebody would see her here.

Stone opened the door with a big smile on his face and said, "That was a short nap. I didn't expect you up so soon."

"I had a wonderful one though." She smiled at him. "Look, something odd just happened. I don't know if it means anything, but I thought I should tell somebody."

He opened the door. "Come inside."

Ice was there, as well as Levi.

She held out her phone and quickly explained. Levi slowly straightened in his chair and said quietly, "Did you recognize his voice?"

Instantly she nodded. "I've spoken to him several times on the phone over the past months," she said. "Even though it's a different phone with more background noise, I still recognized his voice."

"Interesting." Stone brought up the last number she dialed and held it for Ice to see. She wrote it down and then quickly did something on the keyboard.

Lissa looked over and asked, "What are you doing with it, Ice?"

"A search to see if I can find out who owns it."

"Do you think it was him and he just didn't want to acknowledge you?" Stone asked at her side.

It was a rhetorical question as she already knew that's exactly what he had done. "I don't understand why though."

Silence.

Her gaze went from one face to the next. "You think he's involved?"

"We don't think anything at this point," Stone said reassuringly. "But it would be nice to ask him some questions and clear up some issues."

She thought about that and realized she'd like to ask Kevin some of those same ones herself. "Okay, that makes sense. I imagine he'll be doing his damnedest to get another phone as soon as possible if he is involved."

"Of course. We'll do what we can right now. See if we can find out what country he was in when he answered." That came from Ice. "That will tell us a little more."

"Can you do that?"

"I'll make a couple calls. Run down what I can." She

reached for a phone and within seconds spoke to whoever answered the other end.

Stone motioned the two of them out of the small room. Hard for Ice to have a conversation on the phone with other people talking. He shut the door and said, "Not to worry, Lissa. We'll figure this out. How about you go to the kitchen and see if there is any coffee?"

"Sure, that might be nice. If you've got a few minutes, come join me?" she asked Stone.

"I've definitely got some. Has there been any contact from the insurance company yet? Do you need to go to town for anything else?"

"Honestly, I keep my phone off most of the time. I really don't want to deal with very much more right now."

"You just turned it on to call Kevin?"

They walked down the hallway toward the kitchen. "I was planning on contacting some of the other people in the refugee camp. I made a lot of friends there." She looked at him and added, "I remembered that I copied all the numbers down from my old phone while we were on the plane to London." They walked into the kitchen, and she finished with, "I saw Kevin's number and just dialed."

"Nice," he said in an admiring voice.

She shook her head. "I should have tried earlier."

He laughed. "Good job anyway."

In the kitchen he poured two cups of coffee. With her at his side they walked to the small table in front of the windows and sat down.

They hadn't been here for more than a few minutes when Stone's phone went off. He pulled it out and said, "It's Ice. She needs to see me for a few minutes."

Lissa waved him off. "Go. I'll be fine here." He stood

and looked at her. She smiled up at him. "Go."

"Okay, I won't be long." Leaving his coffee cup behind, he strode quickly from the room.

She pulled out her cell and took a look at it, then brought out the napkin with the rest of the numbers on it. It was almost the same as the last one, just updated. She entered the numbers. She put in her father, mother, and then her lawyer's. That was always a good one to put in there. With a smirk she continued to enter the rest. When Marge's came up, she froze as grief overwhelmed her once again.

Surely Kevin couldn't be involved in something so horrible. He was a doctor. He was all about healing, not killing people. And even if he had needed a drug or ingredients to make something of his own creation, why wouldn't he have made alternate plans before?

Maybe Susan had had something to do with it. Lissa considered her quick decline. The fact that the couple's luggage hadn't been with them had Susan asking about it a lot. They had been told it was coming, but it never did.

And Lissa's mind made a giant leap. Maybe it was a good kind of drug. Maybe Susan had a particular disease and the drug kept it at bay. But the minute she couldn't get the next dose, she'd gone downhill quickly—within days. When they had no access to their luggage. By the time they had reached England, still without it, within twenty-four hours she was taken to the hospital. That would also explain why Kevin had disappeared. Because if anybody knew about the drugs, they would've questioned him.

And that meant Lissa needed to talk to the others again. She stood up, grabbed her coffee, and turned around, only to see Stone walk back in again. "There you are," she cried.

He raised his eyebrows. "I was only gone a couple minutes."

She nodded. "I've thought of something else. What's the chance Susan was using the drugs that customs found in my luggage? And without it, she died."

He froze—his mind churning through the possibility. And then with a quick nod he said, "I'll be back in another minute." At the doorway he turned, stopped, and said, "Stay here."

With a laugh she sat down and took another sip. But inside she was feeling much better. They were on the right track. If they could just get a few answers, they could put this to rest. No reason for anybody to still be coming after her.

She looked at the phone, wanting to say something to Kevin. He probably didn't know her luggage never made it to her. If he had been in contact with anybody from Charles's, then he would know the luggage was being held in customs. And now that Susan was dead, what was the point?

Unless the drug had been successful at doing what it was intended to, which is prolonging life and delaying the onset of the disease.

She opened her phone and quickly dialed Kevin again. This time when it rang, it went immediately to voicemail. A computer-automated voice that left no names. She said quickly, "Kevin, my luggage didn't come with me to the States. It was seized by the British authorities. If you're looking for something, I don't have it."

And she hung up, she realized her hands were trembling.

"That's an interesting message," Stone said, standing beside her. He leaned against the wall, his arms crossed over his chest. "Why would you do that?"

She twisted in her seat to face him. "I didn't want him to

think if he hid something in my luggage, there was any chance I still had it."

"Because that also sounded as if you were telling him you lost the package."

Her jaw dropped. "What?" Then she understood and bolted to her feet. "Oh, my God! You can't think I actually knew I was carrying this drug."

"No. It never crossed my mind until I just heard that message you left."

She shook her head emphatically. "I was only trying to tell him to lay off. That if he had hidden something with me, I don't have it."

"Unless he sent it to you another way. More of it perhaps." Stone's intense gaze studied her.

She frowned. "What do you mean, sent it to me?"

He shrugged.

She stared. "He could have, but it would still be sitting in the post office because I haven't been there to grab my mail for the last eight months."

"I thought Marge picked up your mail?"

Lissa frowned and said, "Yes, she did collect what was in the house, but parcels would still be at the post office, wouldn't they?"

"Unless she picked up the notice and took it in to retrieve the packages for you."

"But she'd have to have my ID," she protested.

"Or *somebody* would have to."

She sat back in shock. "Hang on a minute. Are you saying it's possible Marge picked up the mail that could have had a parcel pickup notice in it? And the killer grabbed it and got the package? Or the notice is still sitting in Marge's house?"

Silence came first, then he gave a clipped nod.

"I need my mail anyway. Can we go back and see?" she asked.

"We'll go now." Stone checked his watch and said, "We have a couple hours still left in the business day. I'll tell the others."

She sat quietly. Her thoughts were confused. Did Stone trust her? Or was she really a suspect? And if so, did they actually have any kind of relationship, or was she just fooling herself? Was this some kind of a ploy for her to be kept under close watch in case she slipped up? "In which case, in their minds, I just slipped up," she muttered.

With a heavy heart she walked back to the room she'd just woken up in and grabbed her purse. She caught sight of her single bag of belongings from the day before. She'd added bits and pieces to it and realized how easy it would be to just take it with her right now. She could stay at a hotel overnight. She didn't need to remain here. In fact it was probably better if she left now.

In which case, she should drive her own vehicle so she had her wheels too.

Stone walked into the room behind her. "You ready?"

She turned and picked up the bag of her belongings and said a defiant, "Yes."

At her tone his gaze went to the bag and then to her. "Are you moving out?"

"That's probably a good idea, considering you don't trust me." She took several steps toward the doorway, but he stepped in front of her, crossing his arms, blocking her way.

"And," she added, "maybe you *never* did." She waved her arms around the room behind her. "Maybe this has all been just a sham, making sure you stuck close to *the suspect*."

The look on his face went from shock to incredulous and then he broke into boisterous laughter. He stepped forward, took the bag from her hand, and tossed it on the bed. Then he wrapped his arms around her and tucked her up against his chest.

"I might do a lot of things in the name of getting the job done in order to save somebody else's life," he said, "but I've never slept with anyone because of that. And I wouldn't. Yes, you threw me with that message, but your explanation is also reasonable. These are tough times right now, and we have to consider all possibilities. No, I never thought you were guilty. And, no, I do not think you are now."

She looped her hands behind his back. "You're making me crazy," she wailed. "I used to have a normal life."

He stepped back, then used a finger to tilt up her chin, and said, "You've never had one. But hopefully, when this mess dies down, you'll find out what having one actually means."

HE SHOULDN'T HAVE laughed at her. That wasn't fair. But she'd gotten so defensive, and he realized how she must've taken his questioning earlier. Of course they were going to hurt. But nothing she had said afterward caused concern. He'd always known she was innocent. It just shocked him when he heard the message.

Now he had to do his best to make her believe him, because he did trust her. When he'd first met her, he'd been worried about her lack of interest where her father was concerned for her actions. As if there would be no reprisals. But Stone had come to understand and realized he'd been wrong. She was many things, but unconcerned and heartless weren't two of them.

He reached out and grabbed her hand and said, "Let's go. We don't have too much time to hit the post office before it closes. Have you considered calling the refugee camp to see if any parcels were sent to you there?" He shrugged. "But would anybody have done that without you knowing?"

"Maybe, but I don't know why." She turned her back on him.

"But then it would also mean somebody understood you would be going home, or that someone would be collecting your mail for you."

"Or they thought the latter, and then when we were kidnapped and eventually returned home, they realized there was a change of plans because I was now here."

He studied her face as they walked to the front door. "That's possible." He motioned to the big truck. "We'll take this. Can you call them when we're driving?"

"Sure." As he took them out of the compound and headed toward town, she asked, "Do we need to get permission to go into Marge's house?"

"Levi's working on that." He grinned at the look on her face.

But of course Levi was. They had to look at all angles. They worked with the law, not against it. Unless they were forced to.

His phone rang as he turned onto the main highway. He pulled it from his pocket and clipped it on the dashboard. After pressing the button, he said, "Hey, Levi. What's up?"

"The police say you can go to Marge's. They're okay with her taking any mail that might be there as long as her name is on it. An officer will meet you. Don't enter until he arrives."

"Okay. That's fine. We'll wait for him."

"Also keep an eye out. We're waiting for the officers to transfer our prisoner. You should pass them soon. Can you call me when you see them?"

"Will do."

Stone drove on. Just on the outside of the town's limit, he passed a big black smoke-windowed SUV. He waved at the driver, then leaned across to push Levi's number on his phone. When he answered, Stone said, "Just passed a vehicle now, Levi."

"Thanks. Where are you?"

"At the town's limit."

"Okay, so he's ten minutes out." They could hear Levi talking to somebody in the background. He came back on again and said, "Be careful in town." Then he hung up.

Stone stared at the windshield. He knew exactly what Levi's last words meant, but was hoping Lissa didn't.

He should've known better.

Chapter 22

S HE DIDN'T WANT to ask what particular danger they were facing in town. Her imagination had been running for days as it was. She didn't need any other fuel for that fire. But with Stone beside her, she felt quite confident they'd handle whatever it was.

Hating that sense of impending doom, and being incapable of doing anything about it, she brought out her phone and called the main office in the refugee camp. She hoped Cindy still worked there. They'd been good friends, often spending a fair bit of time together.

"Hello?"

Lissa grinned. "Cindy? Is that you? This is Lissa."

Shocked surprise was followed by an explosive exclamation. "Oh, my God! Lissa, are you all right? We were so worried about you after the kidnapping. We got word you'd been rescued, but that must have been terrible," she cried.

"That's one of the reasons I'm calling," Lissa said. "I wanted to let you know I'm okay. We were rescued from the terrorists, flown to England, now I'm back in the States. All safe and sound."

"Oh, thank God! That was so terrible. We were in shock for days."

"Did you ever increase security after we were kidnapped?"

"Oh, yes, big time. Are Kevin and Susan both okay?" she asked.

"Unfortunately, Susan didn't make it." Lissa's voice dropped in pain. "We got as far as England, but then she died in the hospital there. It looked like she was quite sick. It was something that maybe she didn't know about."

"Oh, no. That's so sad. She was definitely sick. Kevin said she was undergoing constant treatments for some kind of a blood disease."

"Oh, dear. I'm so sorry to hear that. How is it that I didn't know?"

"The only reason I knew was sometimes I had to get Kevin some of the drugs for her. They were really expensive."

"That must've been fun to source out of Afghanistan."

Cindy laughed. "Mostly just mailing stuff to their addresses at one of his houses. And then the drugs were there waiting for them when they got in."

And that brought up a whole mess of new questions. "I didn't even know they had houses." She turned to study Stone, who was paying attention to the road and her conversation.

"I used to mail them out to France and England. They have a house in both places, or that was my understanding."

"Did you send any out recently for him, like before we were kidnapped?"

"Just one to the States." Cindy stopped. Then she said, "I remember now. The last parcel I sent was for you."

"Oh, I totally forgot about the parcel mailed for me." But she turned to look at Stone and shook her head as if to make sure he believed her.

"You probably don't remember because Kevin actually asked me to send it to you for safekeeping. They were coming over for the conference in Houston this week. Remember?"

"Right. With everything going on, it slipped my mind."

"Now that Susan's gone, he may not attend anyway."

"Right, I can ask him. If he wants me to send the box somewhere else, I can do that too."

"When you talk to Kevin, give my condolences. Susan was such a sweetheart."

"That she was."

Lissa hung up after that. Then shared with Stone what was up.

"Interesting. I wonder if that parcel has even arrived yet. It's good news for us if it hasn't."

He pulled the truck up to a stop light. He glanced both ways and then made a left turn. They pulled up in front of Marge's house so fast, she hadn't even realized they were that close.

One of the local officers stood outside waiting for them. They walked up to him slowly. Lissa hooked her arm through Stone's, grateful he was here with her at this house. She did not want to walk in there alone, nor see the devastation again. She knew Marge's body had been taken to the morgue, but she doubted anybody had cleaned up.

She wasn't sure who was responsible for such a thing.

Hopefully the insurance company would step in. She paused at the front door and took a deep breath. It took a moment for her gaze to go past the devastation the intruder had wrought and to think logically about where Marge would've put her mail.

"She said it was in a basket," Lissa said to Stone. They walked in the living room and looked for one on the floor or shelves, but they didn't find anything. They proceeded to the kitchen and took a look around.

On the counter against the rear kitchen door was a small basket with mail in it. Stone lifted it up for her to take a look.

"It seems to be a mix of hers and mine." She kept her eyes averted from the bloodstains on the kitchen floor; the chair appeared to still be in the same position where Marge had been tied up. Lissa went through the mail and pulled out fourteen pieces with her name. Nothing noting parcels waited for her anywhere.

They continued to look through the cupboards for anything else, but it made sense that the basket was where she kept all of it. They replaced it, then turned to the deputy and showed him the mail she had pulled out. She offered her ID to prove who she was, and he let them walk out with it. When they got back into the truck, she rolled down the window and took several deep gulping breaths.

"You okay?"

"I'm not sure I will ever be," she whispered. "Just being in that house—I'd almost blocked it out, but seeing it all over again…"

She felt his hand wrap around hers. He stroked her fingers for a long moment before laying her hand down on her thigh. He cranked the engine. "How do you feel about running past your house? We can check to see if any mail may have arrived today, or since Marge's last visit."

"We might as well. It's on the way to the post office anyway."

"Good enough."

When they pulled up in front of her house five minutes later, her heart sank. This was the last place she wanted to be. On the other hand, with a fast in and out, they might be lucky to find what they were looking for.

Only she stood in the living room fifteen minutes later and realized there was no easy way. They hadn't found anything here. Mail or otherwise.

"Can we leave now?" she asked. She made her way to the front door and opened it. She couldn't wait to get the hell out of here. As far she was concerned, she was never coming back.

He came up behind her, leaving the house together and closing the door. Hearing the door lock, she walked down the steps to the truck. "Do you think anyone's watching us?"

"I don't think so right now. But we will always proceed with caution, with the assumption that it's possible."

They drove down the street to the post office and parked. She sat in the truck for a few minutes, just staring at the front door of the building. "So do I just ask if there is a parcel for me?"

"Does that bother you?"

She shrugged. "It seems odd. Aren't I supposed to have a notice or something?"

He laughed. "I'll do the talking."

"Good." She laughed too. "I like that idea." She hopped out of the truck and fell into step beside him. Inside he headed straight for the front counter.

Without preamble he said, "Good afternoon. Lissa, here," he turned and tugged her forward, wrapping his arm around her shoulder, "just came back from eight months of traveling. She was expecting a parcel, but we haven't seen any sign of it yet. Her friend was collecting her mail, but she has been well, you might have heard, but she was murdered. Her place was trashed. So we have no way of knowing if a notice was left for her to pick up or not." He gave the clerk that damn heartbreaker smile.

The older woman melted. She turned to Lissa. "Oh, you poor dear. What's the last name? I'll go check."

"Brampton," she said quietly. "And thank you."

"No problem. The mail was late today so we have quite a few parcels to sort through." She disappeared into a room in the back.

Stone and Lissa stood silently and waited in the empty store. It was almost closing time.

When the lady didn't return right away, Lissa paced impatiently.

"Well, we found your parcel." The woman came out, carrying a small box. "If you have your ID available, I can confirm it's yours."

Lissa already had it out. The woman checked it, then handed over the box. "There you go."

"While we're here, maybe we can do a change of address form to forward her mail."

"Of course." The postal worker slapped a form down in front of Stone. "Just fill this form out and give it back to me for six months of forwarding."

And then they were done.

As they walked to the truck, the lady walked behind them and locked the post office door.

"Good timing," Stone said as they climbed into the truck.

Lissa didn't say anything. She was still working through his request for the change of address form—and the one he'd written down. It only made sense, considering she wasn't returning to her place and didn't have Marge to pick up any missed mail anymore. It still felt strange. Like a seal of acceptance on her living arrangements with the team, with

Stone.

"You recognize the package?"

She stared down at the simple brown cardboard box. Her name was on the front, but no identifying marks were on it. She checked all the other sides, but nothing indicated where it had come from, other than the stamp that said it was from Afghanistan.

"It's just as Cindy said. But I have no idea what it is." She turned to look at him. "You want to open it here or take it home?"

"Why don't we head down to the coffee shop, and we'll take a look there and then drive home."

HE KNEW HE'D made the right decision by suggesting coffee at the place at the end of the block. It was hardly a date, but it was a few minutes non-work-related away from the others. He had jumped forward and stepped on her toes about forwarding her mail to the compound overruling their earlier decision. But she hadn't protested, although she'd been silent while they were in the truck.

He pulled in and parked, then led her to a small booth at the far end of the restaurant. He ordered coffee for them. "Do you need anything to eat?"

She shook her head. "Alfred's got a big dinner happening. We have time for coffee, but that's about it."

Right. They were working on Alfred's time frame here too. Stone checked his watch and said, "We have half an hour." He brought out his pocketknife and offered it to her.

She shook her head and moved the box closer to him. "For all I know that stuff will explode."

For the merest second, he hesitated and she burst into

cheerful laughter.

He grinned and gently slit the tape open. Flipping open the box, he pulled out another small one with the logo affixed of a very popular and expensive brand-name perfume. Frowning and yet wondering at the same time if this Kevin guy was seriously brilliant or stupid, Stone opened it and found the perfume.

He carefully lifted the bottle from the box and noted the seal around the neck but on closer examination, found it was actually tape, it was well-done.

Replacing the bottle inside, he then repackaged it in the mailing box. He kept it close as he lifted his coffee cup and took a sip, eyeing her over the rim.

He asked the questions burning in the back of his mind. "Where do you see yourself in six months? What do you see yourself doing?"

Startled, she put her cup down and lifted her head to stare at him. "You serious?"

"Yes, I am." And he waited.

"You know, that's not the thing I expected you to ask about." She nudged her chin toward the box. "That's what I was waiting on."

He shrugged. "It's pretty obvious what it is, where it came from, and how it got here. The right answers will come in time." He lowered his cup and added, "What I don't know is what you want. Do you want to go to a friend's house? Be with your family? Or somewhere else? What do you want for yourself?"

"And if I don't have an answer for you?" she asked curiously.

He waited for a moment and then asked, "Don't you have any idea?"

This wasn't exactly going the way he wanted it to. But then they had been falling into a relationship, and he wanted to know that she was invested in this. When he'd seen her grab her bag, ready to move out today, it almost broke his heart. That's when he realized he needed to do something to at least know where he was headed with her.

He didn't want to just travel aimlessly forward into a relationship not really founded on anything other than circumstances. He wanted to know where they stood.

The door to the café opened with force. He glanced over, noting that most of the tables were empty, and caught sight of the man's face and stiffened.

Lissa spun around in her seat and gasped. "Kevin?"

Chapter 23

LISSA STARED IN shock as Kevin walked in the diner and sat down beside her. Then she felt the cold metal of a gun barrel against her ribs, but he never even looked at her. He kept his gaze on Stone. Smart man. Stone would rip him limb from limb for this.

"I'd say it's good to see you, Kevin, but obviously it isn't," she said caustically. "Did you kill your wife?" For the first time she saw a pained look cross his face.

The gun barrel jammed harder into her ribs. "No, you did."

She gasped. "I had nothing to do with it. You can't blame that on me." She shoved her face into his, ignoring the gun barrel's pressure against her ribs. "Besides, it's because of me that you and your wife were rescued."

He glared right back at her. "I needed Susan's bag. The one the kidnappers grabbed. If we'd been able to keep it with us, she'd be alive right now."

She thought about it. "You knew the drugs were in there."

"Of course. It went everywhere with us. Until the kidnapping," he said bitterly.

"But then why do you want it now? And why send it to me?" She motioned to the box. "What difference does it make now? She's dead."

"But I'm not," he spat. "And I have the same damn disease."

"Oh, no!" She stared at him in horror. "Why aren't you getting help then?"

"Have you any idea what that costs? It's not tens of thousands of dollars but hundreds for the treatment. And we don't have any health insurance. We spent the last decade traveling around the world helping people. Keeping everyone else alive. When it came to getting help for ourselves, nobody would cover us. Susan was already sick, and I was showing signs. No insurance company would give us the coverage for pre-existing conditions, for the medicine we needed to keep ourselves alive so we could continue to help others. When it came down to it, nobody cared," he said bitterly. "There's only one treatment, and it was made in Europe. Damn expensive and hard to get a hold of, but I kept digging and digging. Finally I understood how to make it. I have a degree in chemistry and enough knowledge of the body and its systems to create my own. It took several tries, but we had nothing to lose. We were dying anyway. Finally, I found the one that worked. We knew it was no cure, but it slowed the progression." He shrugged. "That was as much as we could hope for. We were looking at having another thirty-plus years this way."

"But that's wonderful. You can make the medicine, save yourself, and give it to the world so others can be helped."

"Anyone who wants it will have to pay for it." He glared at her. "Do you know what it's like to beg for just the basics of a health-care program? It's disgusting. We spent years helping others, and yet nobody would do the same for us. That's what I take away from this. If somebody else wants that goddamn medicine, then they'll have to pay for the treatment."

Not liking what she heard, she sat back. Before her was not the same man she'd worked with for months. Instead she was seeing the bitter hard result of a man who'd fought and lost a war and his wife as a result. "I'm so sorry about Susan," she said. "I had no idea she was sick." She nodded at the box with the perfume in it. "Take it. Take it and go."

"It's not that simple anymore." He turned his fury to Stone. "You involved these men."

"*I* didn't involve anyone. My father hired them to rescue us. We went to the airport to collect our bags, only to be told they were caught up in customs because they found something odd. *Your* drug concoction," she said accusingly.

"Yes, and, if those bags had cleared, I wouldn't have needed the stuff I sent you." He shrugged. "I sent a shipment to my house in France, but it was seized as well. The French officials want to talk to me about it," he said bitterly. "And to top it all off, we've already been paid for the product. And now they want the goods. They want *all* of them."

"But they can't have the stuff from England because it's already been destroyed, and you can't access the shipment in France," Stone said calmly. "So you have this, and nothing else."

Lissa cried out, "Give them what you have and tell them you can make more."

"No. I need this bottle for myself, to stay alive," he snapped, reaching out and snagging up the medicine. "I only came here to get it from your house. You wouldn't even be there, so no harm to anyone. The dealers were supposed to get this, but I can't afford to let them have it now. It will kill me if I do. And they will kill me if I don't. I have to run before they find me. At least until I can collect the ingredients to make more, and that's not so easy to do," he finished in frustration. "It's illegal to import the ingredients. Better I go to the Middle East for them."

"They've already found you, haven't they?" Stone asked.

Lissa stared at Stone. "What do you mean?"

Her gaze went from one to the other. "Stone?"

"Kevin didn't kill Marge. Neither did he trash your place." Stone leaned forward, his face hard. "So someone else knew he was coming here, and he's been one step ahead of Kevin, and been here the whole time." He waited a long moment, then snapped, "Right?"

Kevin frowned. "Yes, damn it. I had told the boss, Harold Jorgenson, about the stash I'd mailed here because I thought I had the other shipments. It would have been so different if I hadn't. He was supposed to keep his eye on the house for it. When Marge showed up to collect the mail, I told him to follow and find out where she lived so he could search her house, but he wasn't supposed to hurt anyone."

"A little late for that, considering Marge is dead," Stone said in a hard voice. "Of course Narque Ltd. has a long history that the authorities are very interested in. We've picked up several minor-league henchmen but there's no guarantee someone higher up the food chain doesn't still want your ass."

Kevin looked slightly relieved, but he didn't ease up the pressure of the gun on her ribs.

She studied his face. "This has been a shit show for days, Kevin. What do you need to do to get out of trouble?"

He turned to her, a light in his eye. "I need money, lots of it. I have to pay them back."

"Just make more and give it to them. Tell them you need another week."

Stone added, "Or however long it takes. If you give them a bit of this supply for them to test, then it will hold them off for a little longer."

"And if you have any of the money left, give him some until you get the rest of the drug made up."

He curled his lip at her.

"Money is not so easily found or handed over." He sneered.

"What choice do you have?" she asked quietly. "You've lost Susan already."

"And Susan failed awfully quickly," Stone added. "Maybe she wasn't reacting the way you thought she would, or maybe the drug doesn't work the way you thought it did."

"That's because she didn't get the next dose," he said in frustration. "If we'd just had that, she would've been fine."

"Are you sure about that?" Because the more she thought about it, the more Lissa wondered if the drug worked at all. Maybe Susan was dying regardless of whatever drug he'd given her. Although Lissa had no proof. "Does it really work?"

He froze.

She leaned forward in shock. "Oh, my God! You took money and promised delivery for a drug that doesn't work."

"It does," he insisted. "It's just Susan was getting accustomed to it. We needed to switch up the dosage and frequency, but we didn't have any more of the drug to do so." He stared out the window, pain in his gaze. "The drug kept her alive for this last year. But like all medication, the body adjusts. I just needed more time. She'd improved so much ..."

"Or it needed more testing and you ran out of both money and time." Stone leaned forward. "Isn't that correct?"

Kevin leaned forward, and the two men glared at each other.

Then suddenly Kevin slumped in his seat. He pulled the gun from her ribs and tucked it into his pocket. "What am I going to do?"

STONE STUDIED THE man across the table from him. Stone hated the fact that Kevin sat beside Lissa. That was the last time Stone would let her sit on the opposite side of the table. It left opportunities like this one. Anger burned inside him for Kevin pulling a gun on Lissa in the first place.

But right now they had to decide how to get out of this mess. "How did you find us?"

With a blank look, Kevin shrugged. "They've been watching for you. They told me to come in and get the drug."

Damn. Stone was afraid of something like that. "Let's get to the compound. Levi can figure this out."

For a moment Kevin looked hopeful, then his face fell. "No, I can't do that."

Stone stood up. He motioned toward the door. "Then I'm taking Lissa home."

Thankfully, all the fight seemed to have left Kevin. He stood up meekly, pocketed the bottle, and walked ahead of them to the front door of the restaurant. Stone held it open with one hand for Lissa. He tossed the empty packaging in a trash can behind the door.

As he stepped out, he heard two hard spits. Kevin's body jerked before collapsing to his knees.

A man raced away from Kevin. The bottle in his hand. He dove into a sedan as it accelerated past the café. Almost for good measure they fired once more. But Stone was already on the move, sending Lissa to the ground and covering her body with his while pushing Kevin all the way to the ground.

Stone felt his shoulder jerk, then heard the vehicle as it screamed off in the distance.

He rolled off Lissa, still swearing a blue streak. Lissa sat up and screamed.

"How bad are you hurt?" she cried. "Oh, my God, they can't keep getting away with this."

"I'm fine, it's just my shoulder." He sat up and glared at the neat hole in his shirt now soaked in blood. "Damn it. I liked this shirt."

She froze, leaned closer, and said, "You really are fine?" Then she grinned. "Well, that was one way to end this."

"Glad you are enjoying yourself." Stone pulled his phone from his pocket and tossed it to her. "Call Levi. Give him an update. Kevin is dead, and the shooter has the medicine. Have Levi let Bullard know too. They were after Kevin all along. Hopefully this ends it. We'll let the authorities deal with Narque Ltd."

In the distance they could hear sirens. Someone had called the cops, so that was done. He lay back on the grass and groaned softly. "This isn't how I had planned our evening."

She kneeled down beside him, ending her call. "Levi and crew are on their way." She picked up his hand. "How did you want it to go?"

He gave a strangled laugh. "I'd planned to discuss our future over coffee and then maybe continue it a little later in bed."

She leaned over and stared into his eyes. "Is that what

you meant about *where do I see myself in six months?*"

"Yes," he whispered. "But you weren't ready to open up."

"I wasn't exactly sure what you were talking about." She kissed him gently on the lips. "But now that I know ..."

"What do you know?"

"That I want to spend the next six months—per my new address notification—with you. Getting to know you, spending my days and my nights with you ..."

He reached up and grabbed her hand. "You have to realize that sometimes my work is dangerous."

"I know." She placed a finger on his lips. "Apparently sometimes mine is too."

"Are you prepared for that?"

"Of course not," she said smoothly. "Who is, until it happens? But what I can tell you is I want to try."

"Are you sure?"

"Absolutely." She grinned and lowered her head. "Surely, with a bum wing, you'll spend the next couple days in bed, right? We do have lots to talk about."

They did at that, and he realized he'd finally found someone he could be himself with. Not just on the good days but on the darker ones too, when life looked gloomy and lonely. It would take a lot for him to open up, but for the first time, he could see himself doing it. Surrendering to what he had with Lissa—in all ways.

A few days in bed? Hell, yes.

"And lots of other things to do?" He grinned at her. "Depending on what you want of course."

"I want one thing and one thing only." She leaned in closer. She whispered against his ear, her warm breath stroking along his neck, sending shudders down his big frame. "Love me, just love me."

His gaze widened, and he twisted so he could see into her eyes, and saw the truth. "That part," he whispered, his heart in his throat, "I can do easily. In fact I already do."

She dropped her forehead gently to his, tears glistening in her eyes. "Thank God. I hated to think I was in this alone."

"I was lost from the start," he murmured. Damn his shoulder. All he wanted to do was hold her close—all night long.

He knew he didn't need it, but he'd do his darnedest to stretch his healing into several days, just so he could stay with her. The guys would understand. They'd bug him about it, but they'd do what they could to give him the time. Life had never looked better.

Epilogue

MERK WOULD MOVE out. That's all there was to it. Or he would insist on every job Levi had out of the damn state—better yet, the country.

The compound had turned into *The Love Boat* on land. Sickening.

There were way too many loving looks and hugging moments for Merk to handle as a single guy. And he knew Sienna had felt the heat too, as had Rhodes. So, okay, Merk wasn't as bad off as he originally thought but still, Legendary Security was getting a name for itself, and he wasn't sure this angle was the type Levi had intended.

He walked past Lissa and Stone sitting at the kitchen table, heads bent together as they made plans. Merk gave a happy sigh. Okay, he was glad for the big guy. Stone had had a much larger hurdle, maybe more than any of them, to finding a permanent relationship. Then again, Lissa was special. And from day one she'd had eyes only for Stone.

They looked so right together.

So did Levi and Ice. Hard to imagine any two people more suited to each other. He knew Mason's unit had been given the moniker Keepers, much to the men's chagrin, but it was seriously true. Now what was Levi doing here? Instead of their nickname, *Heroes for Hire*, it seemed *Heroes for the Heart* sounded a whole lot more appropriate.

Merk shook his head and walked to the living room. Alone, again. He sighed. Sometimes he wished for what the two couples at the compound had, but he had no idea who would be a perfect match for him. He'd had many relationships, but none had worked out.

Then again he had no illusions as to what they were all about. He'd been married once. Not that it counted. How long did a marriage have to last to count? Not that it mattered either; his was over a long time ago. But he'd learned his lesson—and he had no intention of making that mistake again.

Not in this lifetime.

This concludes Book 2 of Heroes for Hire:
Stone's Surrender.
Read about Merk's Mistake: Heroes for Hire, Book 3

Heroes for Hire: Merk's Mistake (Book #3)

Love never fades…

Injuries that require months of lost time are finally a thing of the past, and Merk sails from mission to mission with Legendary Securities, thrilled to be active once more. But when his ex-wife contacts him, panicked and needing his help, he rushes to get to her in time…only to have her snatched away right before his eyes.

When trouble finds her, Katina's first and only thought is her ex-husband Merk. Although they haven't spoken in a decade, nothing about their attraction to each other has changed. If anything, her reaction to him is deeper and stronger than ever before. But, while she reels from all they've lost, her life is on the line and her only focus is staying alive.

Katina has something that others want badly enough to make them risk anything to get, no matter how evil their plan, no matter who they have to kill to get it…

Book 3 is available now!
To find out more visit Dale Mayer's website.
https://geni.us/DMMerkUniversal

Other Military Series by Dale Mayer

SEALs of Honor

Heroes for Hire

SEALs of Steel

The K9 Files

The Mavericks

Bullards Battle

Hathaway House

Terkel's Team

Ryland's Reach: Bullard's Battle
(Book #1)

Welcome to a new stand-alone but interconnected series from Dale Mayer. This is Bullard's story—and that of his team's. All raw, rough, incredibly capable men who have one goal: to find out who was behind the attack on their leader, before the attacker, or attackers, return to finish the job.

Stay tuned for more nonstop action as the men narrow down their suspects … and find a way to let love back into their own empty lives.

His rescue from the ocean after a horrible plane explosion was his top priority, in any way, shape, or form. A small sailboat and a nurse to do the job was more than Ryland hoped for.

When Tabi somehow drags him and his buddy Garret onboard and surprisingly gets them to a naval ship close by, Ryland figures he'd used up all his luck and his friend's too. Sure enough, those who attacked the plane they were in weren't content to let him slowly die in the ocean. No. Surviving had made him a target all over again.

Tabi isn't expecting her sailing holiday to include the rescue of two badly injured men and then to end with the loss of her beloved sailboat. Her instincts save them, but now she finds it tough to let them go—even as more of Bullard's team members come to them—until it becomes apparent that not only are Bullard and his men still targets ... but she is too.

B ULLARD CHECKED THAT the helicopter was loaded with their bags and that his men were ready to leave.

He walked back one more time, his gaze on Ice. She'd never looked happier, never looked more perfect. His heart ached, but he knew she remained a caring friend and always would be. He opened his arms; she ran into them, and he held her close, whispering, "The offer still stands."

She leaned back and smiled up at him. "Maybe if and when Levi's been gone for a long enough time for me to forget," she said in all seriousness.

"That's not happening. You two, now three, will live long and happy lives together," he said, smiling down at the woman knew to be the most beautiful, inside and out. She would never be his, but he always kept a little corner of his heart open and available, in case she wanted to surprise him and to slide inside.

And then he realized she'd already been a part of his heart all this time. That was a good ten to fifteen years by now. But she kept herself in the friend category, and he understood because she and Levi, partners and now parents, were perfect together.

Bullard reached out and shook Levi's hand. "It was a hell of a blast," he said. "When you guys do a big splash, you really do a *big* splash."

Ice laughed. "A few days at home sounds perfect for me now."

"It looks great," he said, his hands on his hips as he surveyed the people in the massive pool surrounded by the palm trees, all designed and decked out by Ice. Right beside all the war machines that he heartily approved of. He grinned at her. "When are you coming over to visit?" His gaze went to Levi, raising his eyebrows back at her. "You guys should come over for a week or two or three."

"It's not a bad idea," Levi said. "We could use a long holiday, just not yet."

"That sounds familiar." Bullard grinned. "Anyway, I'm off. We'll hit the airport and then pick up the plane and head home." He added, "As always, call if you need me."

Everybody raised a hand as he returned to the helicopter and his buddy who was flying him to the airport. Ice had volunteered to shuttle him there, but he hadn't wanted to take her away from her family or to prolong the goodbye. He hopped inside, waving at everybody as the helicopter lifted. Two of his men, Ryland and Garret, were in the back seats. They always traveled with him.

Bullard would pick up the rest of his men in Australia. He stared down at the compound as he flew overhead. He preferred his compound at home, but damn they'd done a nice job here.

With everybody on the ground screaming goodbye, Bullard sailed over Houston, heading toward the airport. His two men never said a word. They all knew how he felt about Ice. But not one of them would cross that line and say anything. At least not if they expected to still have jobs.

It was one thing to fall in love with another man's woman, but another thing to fall in love with a woman who was so unique, so different, and so absolutely perfect that you knew, just knew, there was no hope of finding anybody else like her. But she and Levi had been together way before Bullard had ever met her, which made it that much more heartbreaking.

Still, he'd turned and looked forward. He had a full roster of jobs himself to focus on when he got home. Part of him was tired of the life; another part of him couldn't wait to head out on the next adventure. He managed to run everything from his command centers in one or two of his locations. He'd spent a lot of time and effort at the second one and kept a full team at both locations, yet preferred to spend most of his time at the old one. It felt more like home to him, and he'd like to be there now, but still had many more days before that could happen.

The helicopter lowered to the tarmac, he stepped out, said his goodbyes and walked across to where his private plane waited. It was one of the things that he loved, being a pilot of both helicopters and airplanes, and owning both birds himself.

That again was another way he and Ice were part of the same team, of the same mind-set. He'd been looking for another woman like Ice for himself, but no such luck. Sure, lots were around for short-term relationships, but most of them couldn't handle his lifestyle or the violence of the world that he lived in. He understood that.

The ones who did had a hard edge to them that he found difficult to live with. Bullard appreciated everybody's being alert and aware, but if there wasn't some softness in the women, they seemed to turn cold all the way through.

As he boarded his small plane, Ryland and Garret following behind, Bullard called out in his loud voice, "Let's go, slow pokes. We've got a long flight ahead of us."

The men grinned, confident Bullard was teasing, as was his usual routine during their off-hours.

"Well, we're ready, not sure about you though ..." Ryland said, smirking.

"We're waiting on you this time," Garret added with a chuckle. "Good thing you're the boss."

Bullard grinned at his two right-hand men. "Isn't that the truth?" He dropped his bags at one of the guys' feet and said, "Stow all this stuff, will you? I want to get our flight path cleared and get the hell out of here."

They'd all enjoyed the break. He tried to get over once a year to visit Ice and Levi and same in reverse. But it was time to get back to business. He started up the engines, got confirmation from the tower. They were heading to Australia for this next job. He really wanted to go straight back to Africa, but it would be a while yet. They'd refuel in Honolulu.

Ryland came in and sat down in the copilot's spot, buckled in, then asked, "You ready?"

Bullard laughed. "When have you ever known me *not* to be ready?" At that, he taxied down the runway. Before long he was up in the air, at cruising level, and heading to Hawaii. "Gotta love these views from up here," Bullard said. "This place is magical."

"It is once you get up above all the smog," he said. "Why Australia again?"

"Remember how we were supposed to check out that newest compound in Australia that I've had my eye on? Besides the alpha team is coming off that ugly job in Sydney. We'll give them a day or two of R&R then head home."

"Right. We could have some equally ugly payback on that job."

Bullard shrugged. "That goes for most of our jobs. It's the life."

"And don't you have enough compounds to look after?"

"Yes I do, but that kid in me still looks to take over the world. Just remember that."

"Better you go home to Africa and look after your first two compounds," Ryland said.

"Maybe," Bullard admitted. "But it seems hard to not continue expanding."

"You need a partner," Ryland said abruptly. "That might ease the savage beast inside. Keep you home more."

"Well, the only one I like," he said, "is married to my best friend."

"I'm sorry about that," Ryland said quietly. "What a shit deal."

"No," Bullard said. "I came on the scene last. They were always meant to be together. Especially now they are a family."

"If you say so," Ryland said.

Bullard nodded. "Damn right, I say so."

And that set the tone for the next many hours. They landed in Hawaii, and while they fueled up everybody got off to stretch their legs by walking around outside a bit as this was a small private airstrip, not exactly full of hangars and tourists. Then they hopped back on board again for takeoff.

"I can fly," Ryland offered as they took off.

"We'll switch in a bit," Bullard said. "Surprisingly, I'm doing okay yet, but I'll let you take her down."

"Yeah, it's still a long flight," Ryland said studying the islands below. It was a stunning view of the area.

"I love the islands here. Sometimes I just wonder about the benefit of, you know, crashing into the sea, coming up on a deserted island, and finding the simple life again," Bullard said with a laugh.

"I hear you," Ryland said. "Every once in a while, I wonder the same."

Several hours later Ryland looked up and said abruptly, "We've made good time considering we've already passed Fiji."

Bullard yawned.

"Let's switch."

Bullard smiled, nodded, and said, "Fine. I'll hand it over to you."

Just then a funny noise came from the engine on the right side.

They looked at each other, and Ryland said, "Uh-oh. That's not good news."

Boom!

And the plane exploded.

Find Bullard's Battle (Book #1) here!
To find out more visit Dale Mayer's website.
https://geni.us/DMRylandUniversal

Damon's Deal: Terkel's Team (Book #1)

Welcome to a brand-new connected series of intrigue, betrayal, and … murder, from the *USA Today* best-selling author Dale Mayer. A series with all the elements you've come to love, plus so much more… including psychics!

A betrayal from within has Terkel frantic to protect those he can, as his team falls one by one, from a murderous killer he helped create.

ICE POURED HERSELF a coffee and sat down at the compound's massive dining room table with the others. When her phone rang, she smiled at the number displayed. "Hey, Terk. How're you doing?" She put the call on Speakerphone.

"I'm okay," Terkel said, his voice distracted and tight.

"Terk?" Merk called from across the table. He got up and walked closer and sat across from Levi. "You don't sound too good, brother. What's up?"

"I'm fine," Terk said. "Or I will be. Right now, things are blown to shit."

"As in literally?" Merk asked.

"The entire group," Terk said, "they're all gone. I had a solid team of eight, and they're all gone."

"Dead?"

Several others stood to join them, gathered around Ice's phone. Levi stepped forward, his hand on Ice's shoulder. "Terk? Are they all dead?"

"No." Terk took a deep breath. "I'm not making sense. I'm sorry."

"Take it easy," Ice said, her voice calm and reassuring. "What do you mean, *they're all gone?*"

"All their abilities are gone," he said. "Something's happened to them. Somebody has deliberately removed whatever super senses they could utilize—or what we have been utilizing for the last ten years for the government." His tone was bitter. "When the US gov recently closed us down, they promised that our black ops department would never rise again, but I didn't expect them to attack us personally."

"What are you talking about?" Merk said in alarm, standing up now to stare at Ice's phone. "Are you in danger?"

"Maybe? I don't know," Terk said. "I need to find out exactly what the hell's going on."

"What can we do to help?" Ice asked.

Terk gave a broken laugh. "That's not why I'm calling. Well, it is, but it isn't."

Ice looked at Merk, who frowned, as he shook his head. Ice knew he and the others had heard Terk's stressed out tone and the completely confusing bits and pieces coming from his mouth. Ice said, "Terk, you're not making sense again. Take a breath and explain. Please. You're scaring me."

Terk took a long slow deep breath. "Tell Stone to open the gate," he said. "She's out there."

"Who's out there?" Levi asked, hopped up, looked outside, and shrugged.

"She's coming up the road now. You have to let her in."

"Who? Why?"

"*Because*," he said, "she's also harnessed with C-4."

"Jesus," Levi said, bolting to display the camera feeds to the big screen in the room. "Is it live?"

"It is, and she's been sent to you."

"Well, that's an interesting move," Ice said, her voice sharp, activating her comm to connect to Stone in the control room. "Who's after us?"

"I think it's rebels within the Iranian government. But it could be our own government. I don't know anymore," Terk snapped. "I also don't know how they got her so close to you. Or how they pinned your connection to me," he said. "I've been very careful."

"We can look after ourselves," Ice said immediately. "But who is this woman to you?"

"She's pregnant," he said, "so that adds to the intensity here."

"Understood. So who is the father? Is he connected somehow?"

There was silence on the other end.

Merk said, "Terk, talk to us."

"She's carrying my baby," Terk replied, his voice heavy.

Merk, his expression grim, looked at Ice, her face mirroring his shock. He asked, "How do you know her, Terk?"

"Brother, you don't understand," Terk said. "I've never met this woman before in my life." And, with that, the phone went dead.

Find Terkel's Team (Book #1) here!

To find out more visit Dale Mayer's website.

https://geni.us/DMTTDamonUniversal

Author's Note

Thank you for reading Stone's Surrender: Heroes for Hire, Book 2! If you enjoyed the book, please take a moment and leave a short review.

Dear reader,

I love to hear from readers, and you can contact me at my website: www.dalemayer.com or at my Facebook author page. To be informed of new releases and special offers, sign up for my newsletter or follow me on BookBub. And if you are interested in joining Dale Mayer's Reader Group, here is the Facebook sign up page.
http://geni.us/DaleMayerFBGroup

Cheers,
Dale Mayer

About the Author

Dale Mayer is a *USA Today* best-selling author, best known for her SEALs military romances, her Psychic Visions series, and her Lovely Lethal Garden cozy series. Her contemporary romances are raw and full of passion and emotion (Broken But ... Mending, Hathaway House series). Her thrillers will keep you guessing (Kate Morgan, By Death series), and her romantic comedies will keep you giggling (*It's a Dog's Life*, a stand-alone novella; and the Broken Protocols series, starring Charming Marvin, the cat).

Dale honors the stories that come to her—and some of them are crazy, break all the rules and cross multiple genres!

To go with her fiction, she also writes nonfiction in many different fields, with books available on résumé writing, companion gardening, and the US mortgage system. All her books are available in print and ebook format.

Connect with Dale Mayer Online

Dale's Website – www.dalemayer.com
Twitter – @DaleMayer
Facebook Page – geni.us/DaleMayerFBFanPage
Facebook Group – geni.us/DaleMayerFBGroup
BookBub – geni.us/DaleMayerBookbub
Instagram – geni.us/DaleMayerInstagram
Goodreads – geni.us/DaleMayerGoodreads
Newsletter – geni.us/DaleNews

Also by Dale Mayer

Published Adult Books:

Bullard's Battle

Ryland's Reach, Book 1

Cain's Cross, Book 2

Eton's Escape, Book 3

Garret's Gambit, Book 4

Kano's Keep, Book 5

Fallon's Flaw, Book 6

Quinn's Quest, Book 7

Bullard's Beauty, Book 8

Bullard's Best, Book 9

Terkel's Team

Damon's Deal, Book 1

Kate Morgan

Simon Says… Hide, Book 1

Hathaway House

Aaron, Book 1

Brock, Book 2

Cole, Book 3

Denton, Book 4

The K9 Files

Harley, Book 14

The K9 Files, Books 1–2

The K9 Files, Books 3–4

The K9 Files, Books 5–6

The K9 Files, Books 7–8

The K9 Files, Books 9–10

The K9 Files, Books 11–12

Lovely Lethal Gardens

Arsenic in the Azaleas, Book 1

Bones in the Begonias, Book 2

Corpse in the Carnations, Book 3

Daggers in the Dahlias, Book 4

Evidence in the Echinacea, Book 5

Footprints in the Ferns, Book 6

Gun in the Gardenias, Book 7

Handcuffs in the Heather, Book 8

Ice Pick in the Ivy, Book 9

Jewels in the Juniper, Book 10

Killer in the Kiwis, Book 11

Lifeless in the Lilies, Book 12

Murder in the Marigolds, Book 13

Lovely Lethal Gardens, Books 1–2

Lovely Lethal Gardens, Books 3–4

Lovely Lethal Gardens, Books 5–6

Lovely Lethal Gardens, Books 7–8

Lovely Lethal Gardens, Books 9–10

Psychic Vision Series

Tuesday's Child

Hide 'n Go Seek

Maddy's Floor

Garden of Sorrow

Knock Knock…

Rare Find

Eyes to the Soul

Now You See Her

Shattered

Into the Abyss

Seeds of Malice

Eye of the Falcon

Itsy-Bitsy Spider

Unmasked

Deep Beneath

From the Ashes

Stroke of Death

Ice Maiden

Snap, Crackle…

Psychic Visions Books 1–3

Psychic Visions Books 4–6

Psychic Visions Books 7–9

By Death Series

Touched by Death

Haunted by Death

Chilled by Death

By Death Books 1–3

Broken Protocols – Romantic Comedy Series

Cat's Meow

Cat's Pajamas

Cat's Cradle

Cat's Claus

Broken Protocols 1-4

Broken and... Mending

Skin

Scars

Scales (of Justice)

Broken but... Mending 1-3

Glory

Genesis

Tori

Celeste

Glory Trilogy

Biker Blues

Morgan: Biker Blues, Volume 1

Cash: Biker Blues, Volume 2

SEALs of Honor

Mason: SEALs of Honor, Book 1

Hawk: SEALs of Honor, Book 2

Dane: SEALs of Honor, Book 3

Swede: SEALs of Honor, Book 4

Shadow: SEALs of Honor, Book 5

Cooper: SEALs of Honor, Book 6

Heroes for Hire

Levi's Legend: Heroes for Hire, Book 1

Stone's Surrender: Heroes for Hire, Book 2

Merk's Mistake: Heroes for Hire, Book 3

Rhodes's Reward: Heroes for Hire, Book 4

Flynn's Firecracker: Heroes for Hire, Book 5

Logan's Light: Heroes for Hire, Book 6

Harrison's Heart: Heroes for Hire, Book 7

Saul's Sweetheart: Heroes for Hire, Book 8

Dakota's Delight: Heroes for Hire, Book 9

Michael's Mercy (Part of Sleeper SEAL Series)

Tyson's Treasure: Heroes for Hire, Book 10

Jace's Jewel: Heroes for Hire, Book 11

Rory's Rose: Heroes for Hire, Book 12

Brandon's Bliss: Heroes for Hire, Book 13

Liam's Lily: Heroes for Hire, Book 14

North's Nikki: Heroes for Hire, Book 15

Anders's Angel: Heroes for Hire, Book 16

Reyes's Raina: Heroes for Hire, Book 17

Dezi's Diamond: Heroes for Hire, Book 18

Vince's Vixen: Heroes for Hire, Book 19

Ice's Icing: Heroes for Hire, Book 20

Johan's Joy: Heroes for Hire, Book 21

Galen's Gemma: Heroes for Hire, Book 22

Zack's Zest: Heroes for Hire, Book 23

Bonaparte's Belle: Heroes for Hire, Book 24

Heroes for Hire, Books 1–3

Heroes for Hire, Books 4–6

Heroes for Hire, Books 7–9

Heroes for Hire, Books 10–12

Heroes for Hire, Books 13–15

SEALs of Steel

Badger: SEALs of Steel, Book 1

Erick: SEALs of Steel, Book 2

Cade: SEALs of Steel, Book 3

Talon: SEALs of Steel, Book 4

Laszlo: SEALs of Steel, Book 5

Geir: SEALs of Steel, Book 6

Jager: SEALs of Steel, Book 7

The Final Reveal: SEALs of Steel, Book 8

SEALs of Steel, Books 1–4

SEALs of Steel, Books 5–8

SEALs of Steel, Books 1–8

The Mavericks

Kerrick, Book 1

Griffin, Book 2

Jax, Book 3

Beau, Book 4

Asher, Book 5

Ryker, Book 6

Miles, Book 7

Nico, Book 8

Keane, Book 9

Lennox, Book 10

Gavin, Book 11

Shane, Book 12

Diesel, Book 13

Jerricho, Book 14

The Mavericks, Books 1–2

The Mavericks, Books 3–4

The Mavericks, Books 5–6

The Mavericks, Books 7–8

The Mavericks, Books 9–10

The Mavericks, Books 11–12

Collections

Dare to Be You…

Dare to Love…

Dare to be Strong…

RomanceX3

Standalone Novellas

It's a Dog's Life

Riana's Revenge

Second Chances

Published Young Adult Books:

Family Blood Ties Series

Vampire in Denial

Vampire in Distress

Vampire in Design

Vampire in Deceit

Vampire in Defiance

Vampire in Conflict

Vampire in Chaos

Vampire in Crisis

Vampire in Control

Vampire in Charge

Family Blood Ties Set 1–3

Family Blood Ties Set 1–5

Family Blood Ties Set 4–6

Family Blood Ties Set 7–9

Sian's Solution, A Family Blood Ties Series Prequel Novelette

Design series

Dangerous Designs

Deadly Designs

Darkest Designs

Design Series Trilogy

Standalone

In Cassie's Corner

Gem Stone (a Gemma Stone Mystery)

Time Thieves

Published Non-Fiction Books:

Career Essentials

Career Essentials: The Résumé

Career Essentials: The Cover Letter

Career Essentials: The Interview

Career Essentials: 3 in 1

www.ingramcontent.com/pod-product-compliance
Lightning Source LLC
Chambersburg PA
CBHW071516110726
47908CB00003B/860